To Gary + Leslie,
Enjoy! Best Wishes,
Peter

A Moment of Passion

BY: PETER G. ENGELMAN

This is a work of fiction. The characters, incidents and dialogue are products of the author's imagination and are not to be construed as real. Where the names of actual people, living or dead, are used, the situations, incidents and dialogue concerning those persons are entirely fictional and are not intended to depict any actual events or change the entirely fictional nature of the work.

A Moment of Passion, a fictional novel By Peter G. Engelman, ISBN-10: 0-9744277-4-8, ISBN-13: 978-0-97442-774-4, Published 2006 by Terumah Publishing, 5 Pipe Hill Court, Unit C, Baltimore, MD 21209 © Peter G. Engelman. All rights reserved. No part of this publication may be reproduced, stored in a retrieval system, or transmitted in any form or by any means, electronic, mechanical or otherwise, without the prior written permission of Peter G. Engelman. Front cover photo, *Kissing You* © Paulus Rusyanto, Ximagination, Image from BigStockPhoto.com. Rear cover design by Peter G. Engelman, Terumah Publishing. Orders can be fulfilled from publisher's web site at **www.terumah.com** or from order form in rear of book.

Printed in the United States of America

This book is dedicated to my son, Steven, who has proven to be the bravest and most giving person I have ever met.

Acknowledgements

I wish to thank my neighbors, Linda and Ed Schwartzman for their encouragement and interest in my literary work and achievements. As avid readers, their constructive feedback was invaluable to me. I also want to thank my dear friend, Eileen Lesser, for her proofing and editing help. Finally, I wish to thank my wonderful wife and soul mate, Sandy, for her support and continuing devotion to me during the many hours spent at this endeavor.

Preface

There are limited themes in the world of writing, particularly in the romance genre. The saying, "Love makes the world go round," is a wonderful expression for romance writers because it says so much in such few words. In the end, all love stories are simply variations of the "love chase" embellished by sub-plots.

The theme of this story is familiar: older teacher falls in love with younger student; younger student falls in love with older teacher. The "hook," if you will, is that the relationship is flawed from the onset and appears destined to fail. The main character, Katrina Cole, a student at Willamette University, suffers with emotional illness as a result of an abusive relationship with her widowed father. Named after the horrific August 2005 hurricane that almost wiped New Orleans off the map, Katrina, like the once thriving metropolis, is left empty and scarred, unable to achieve a healthy romantic relationship.

The story begins in Salem, Oregon, a rich fertile region of our country, where Native Americans once roamed and ruled this land of milk and honey. Laura Sunshine, a half-breed Kalupuya Indian is Katie's best friend and confidant. She is endowed with special understandings of the heart and uses her gifts to help Katie maintain her emotional balance. Their unique relationship supports the central love theme in a way that keeps the reader wanting more.

Peter G. Engelman

Table of Contents

Chapter 1 – Friends

Katrina Cole was raised by her widowed father, Jacob, a.k.a. Jack (King) Cole, a lumberjack, who lived and died working at a sawmill in Salem, Oregon.

The city of Salem, named after the Hebrew word *Shalom*, meaning peace, is located in the Willamette Valley, a fertile area that was originally inhabited by Kalupuya Indians. Although the Native Americans were moved to reservations along the coast, 20 years before the Civil War, their mark was indelibly engraved on the area. Many of the natural hunting and fishing sanctuaries in the Valley bear Kalupuya names and their 10,000-year-old history is part of the land.

The city, which is the capital of the state, has a population of around 140,000 and is either second or third largest of the state, depending on the census date.

Katie didn't spend much time in the city. She lived with her father on the outskirts of town, in a small four-room cottage, just a mile from the sawmill.

She attended missionary schools for her primary education. The schools were built along the Willamette River to accommodate the children of families involved in the timber industry. Her first experience with education was in The Mill Creek Mission, a small church with a side addition housing two classrooms. The main chapel served about 50 families, mostly loggers, and vacationers that owned small cottages either in the secluded woodland or in nearby neighborhoods.

As an only child, the lumberjack's daughter had a cloistered life. She spent her days in school and her evenings doing homework and keeping house for her widowed father. On the weekends, she would visit the city with her dad helping him shop for groceries.

Katie's only friend was a dark-haired Indian girl, named Laura Sunshine. Laura, who was half Kalupuya, lived about a mile down the river. The two met in first grade and continued their friendship through high school. During their early years together, Laura taught her friend the ways of the Indian and some of their ancient customs and beliefs. Katie loved hearing of the folklore and it made Laura feel special to pass it on.

In their free time, the girls would take nature walks together. Laura would point out and name some of the medicinal herbs that grew naturally in the plush forest; plants that her father, a full-blooded Kalupuya, had harvested and put to use whenever someone was ill. She used Indian names to describe the therapeutic foliage and over time, Katie learned to recognize and reap the benefits of the curative leaves and roots.

Laura's knowledge of Indian practices fascinated Katie and she wanted to know more. On Saturdays, when she visited the city with her father, she would make stops at the library and borrow books on the subject. After a while, she became an authority on American Indian tribes and often surprised Laura with her knowledge.

The years passed and the girls continued their close friendship.

Katie had just started her second year of college when the accident at the mill occurred. Jack was working his regular job gaffing the logs down the waterway into the feeding troughs. Jam-ups were normal as the timber made its way down the river and with over 20 years of experience, Jack knew which logs were key to freeing the pack. This day was different. The logjam appeared normal to the eye but beneath the pile, a rogue log lay hidden like a crocodile in wait. When Jack gaffed the key log, the sudden release of pressure sent the secluded log airborne. In less than a second, the 3-ton wooden projectile hit Jack square in the chest killing him instantly.

Chapter 2 – Saying Goodbye

The funeral service for Jacob Cole was held three days after the accident, at the Simpson Funeral Home on Green Street.

The sky was gray and it was raining heavily that morning, but it didn't deter some 40 co-workers from saying goodbye to their good friend.

Fred Thompson, pastor of the Mill Creek Church officiated. Fred was a familiar face to the congregants. Besides preaching on Sunday mornings at the riverside church, he also worked at the mill, in quality control.

Jack Cole was laid out in a polished casket made of Western red cedar. The coffin, which was paid for by the sawmill, was seemingly made from treated lumber that Jack had gaffed at one time or another.

Pastor Thompson stood at a 3-foot lectern with a ragged King James Version of the Bible in his right hand. Looking down from the raised pulpit, the preacher gazed at the last remains of his co-worker and parishioner. The minister began his eulogy.

"Jacob, Jack King Cole," the clergyman waited for the chuckles to subside, "was indeed a merry old soul. He was also a dear friend and a skilled lumberjack. Jack and I go way back, probably 20 years or more. When he and Jenny called on me to marry them, I was honored. I remember how very much they loved each other and how affectionate they were to one another the day of their wedding.

"Two years later, I was delighted to hear that Jenny was going to give birth. But, when Jack called me a few months later and asked me to come to the hospital, I was deeply concerned. I knew something was wrong as soon as I heard Jack's frail voice over the phone.

"When I arrived at the hospital," Fred took a deep breath. He looked to the first row of seats where Katie sat grieving.

"Jack greeted me with tears streaming down his cheeks. I can still hear his first words. He was so distraught he could barely speak. He said to me 'Katie, Katie is so beautiful.' Folks, can you believe this? Here was a man whose life was coming apart at the seams – a man whose wife was dying, hanging on to life by only a thread, but Jack focused on the positive – he had the little girl he always wanted.

5

"After telling me about you Katie, he went on, talking to me about your mother and how she had hemorrhaged during the delivery." The preacher looked straight at Katie and his eyes glistened with his own tears as he recalled the event.

"Katie, your mother and father were special people. They didn't have much time together as husband and wife, but they created a beautiful legacy in you."

The minister gathered himself trying to throw off the emotions that were impeding his speech. He looked past Katie into the eyes of his audience and saw that they too were moved by his words.

"Jack Cole was a man of stature. He was a strong man, both physically and spiritually. He stood 6-feet-2-inches tall, a giant of a man, like the trees he felled. But, like those lofty timbers, he was cut down in the prime of his life. We will all remember Jack Cole as we say our last good-bye's and we will cherish his memory forever in the name of our Lord, Jesus Christ."

Pastor Thompson opened his Bible to a book-marked page and concluded the short service by asking the congregation to join in the reading of the 23rd Psalm.

'The Lord is my Shepherd; I shall not want.

He maketh me to lie down in green pastures:

He leadeth me beside the still waters.

He restoreth my soul:

He leadeth me in the paths of righteousness for His name' sake.

Yea, though I walk through the valley of the
shadow of death,

I will fear no evil: For thou art with me;

Thy rod and thy staff, they comfort me.

Thou preparest a table before me in the presence of
mine enemies;

Thou annointest my head with oil; My cup runneth
over.

Surely goodness and mercy shall follow me all the
days of my life,

and I will dwell in the House of the Lord forever.'

The sorrowful preacher closed his Bible and
thanked everyone for attending. He stepped down from
the pulpit and after hugging Katie, shook hands and
chatted with his parishioners.

Chapter 3 – Moving on

Willamette University, known as the first university in the West, was founded in 1842 as a school for children of missionaries. The campus, located in downtown Salem, has a student population of about 2,500 and sits directly across from the State Capitol.

Katie, who elected to major in history, received a full four-year scholarship from the college. Her friend, Laura Sunshine, was not as fortunate. Her grades were not as good and her family couldn't afford the tuition of the prestigious institution. After high school, Laura enrolled in a 12-month beautician's course at the Salem School of Cosmetology. Upon completion, she took a job with a beauty salon on the West Side of town.

The sudden unexpected death of Jack Cole, left Katie devastated. Her father was the bedrock of her life; her entire routine revolved around him. Returning to an empty house every day, eating dinner alone and having no one to share her day, left her depressed and lonely. The freckled face that normally carried a smile was laden with sorrow. Normally an "A" student, the orphaned teen began falling back on her grades. What was once challenging and interesting became boring and mundane. The second semester of her sophomore year was a total collapse. Katie's "A" average dropped to a "C" and she was in danger of losing her scholarship.

Franklin Hardgrove was new to Willamette and was serving out his second term in the Guidance Department. Hardgrove had come to Salem from the East after graduating from the University of Virginia in Charlottesville. He held both Bachelor's and Master's degrees in Education and was enjoying his popularity with the students. The young 24-year-old bachelor lived in a small one-bedroom apartment just a mile from the university.

When Katie lost her father and her grades began to slip, her class advisor arranged an appointment with the accredited counselor. Katie walked into Hardgrove's office sullen and emotional. Her fair skin, which generally carried a warm glow, was pale; her gait was noticeably sluggish. She carried a knapsack of books over her right shoulder. As she entered the room, she removed the heavy canvas bag and lowered it to the floor.

"Hi, I'm Franklin Hardgrove," the good looking counselor said, standing and holding out his hand.

"Please take a seat, make yourself comfortable," he said, shaking the clammy hand that barely acknowledged his own. He held the slender fingers a little longer than customary for a handshake but didn't know why.

Katie looked at the white-framed diplomas on the wall while the bow-tied counselor took his seat.

"I understand that you recently lost your father," Hardgrove said empathetically. I'm sorry. I heard about the accident."

Katie looked up at the young guidance teacher her damp eyes glistening. Through her blurred lenses she noticed the piercing blue eyes of the man the girls called "Hottie."

"I'm sorry," she uttered, wiping her tears with a tissue.

"Don't be, I know exactly how you feel. I lost my dad a year ago."

"My father was my whole life," Katie sobbed. I can't seem to get it together since…" she stopped in mid sentence.

"Maybe I can help," Hardgrove said, passing Katie another tissue.

***

Laura and Katie continued their friendship through high school, but their physical contact waned when Laura became socially active and began dating. Katie had other things on her mind besides boys. She had more than her share of offers, even more so when she entered college, but she never accepted a single one, for she regarded her responsibilities at home as primary and equated dating with unfaithfulness to her father.

Laura on the other hand was not faced with the same burden. Both of her parents were alive and well. She began dating in the ninth grade. By the time of her graduation, she was seriously involved with a Jewish lawyer who was deeply attracted to the dark-skinned half-breed.

Sam Vollenstein, a graduate of The University of Oregon law school, was five-years older than Laura. Right out of college, he joined the eminent law firm of Winner and Grady, With ten partners and 20 associates, the firm was one of the largest in the State. By his third year with the firm, Sam was already in line for a partnership.

Money came easy to the young attorney. He maintained an upscale apartment in one of Salem's finest suburbs and drove a fancy sports car. Acting against her parent's wishes, Laura moved in with the aspiring lawyer.

Her new lover and his rapid ascent to wealth smote the Kalupuya beauty. She saw in him an opportunity to escape from the economic and racial discrimination she and her family suffered because of their cultural heritage.

Later, she would come to realize that the glamorous life she envisioned with Sam was anything but rewarding.

Chapter 4 – Healing

Katie and her male counselor met every Tuesday afternoon between 2 and 3 p.m. The time was convenient for Katie as her last class ended an hour before. It gave her some downtime to complete her homework assignments. Hardgrove reserved the time as his last session of the day.

At first, the discussions centered on Katie's grief and her feelings of loss. Hardgrove allowed his patient wide latitude with her feelings encouraging her to speak frankly.

As the meetings progressed, Katie began to express some of her deep-rooted feelings. She spoke of her lonely home life and the guilt she felt whenever she left her father alone.

"My mother died in childbirth," she confided.

13

"My father raised me himself; I always felt like I owed him for that."

Hardgrove interrupted.

"But your mother's death wasn't your fault; I'm sure your father didn't hold you responsible."

"Well, he never said it was my fault, but his actions suggested something else."

"What do you mean?"

"Well the way he treated me. He made me feel that I owed him because of my mother dying in childbirth. I remember always doing for him: cooking and laundry and cleaning house. He never told me to do it, but he never told me *not to*. I guess it's partly my fault because I never complained to him. I always felt like I had to do it because my mother wasn't around."

"What about friends? Do you have any social acquaintances?"

"I have one good friend. Her name is Laura Sunshine; she's half-Indian...we still keep in touch, but not like we used to. She's involved with a guy...lives with him. Growing up, we were best of friends"

"What about boys?" Hardgrove asked. "Have you had any male relationships?"

"No, I never had the time or interest; besides, my father wouldn't approve."

"Why is that?" Hardgrove asked.

"After my mother died, my father never dated. He used to say, 'it wasn't right.' I guess I felt obligated to do the same."

Hardgrove sat back in his chair and thought about his client's response. *Why is she so self-sacrificing, there must be more?*

"Katie, your father is gone. He can't judge you any more. You are a beautiful young lady with your whole life ahead of you. Don't you think you are entitled to a life?"

The counselor's question touched an emotional nerve bringing tears to the student's eyes. Hardgrove sat silent, gazing at the 19-year-old, taking in her soft features and feeling her innocence and sadness. Suddenly a pristine stream of autumn sun looking for a place to lay its beam burst through the office window, illuminating Katie's long auburn hair. Hardgrove watched the sudden aberration of light encircle the soft face in front of him. The advisor was awed by the curiosity. *My God*, he thought, *she looks like an angel.*

Aware of the lag in conversation, Katie stirred nervously in her chair. The strong sunlight filled her face with a blinding brilliance. The combination of tears and light blurred her eyes; she couldn't see Hardgrove's face, but felt his penetrating blue eyes on her. She blotted her wet eyes and lowered her head in embarrassment.

Hardgrove, sensing her discomfort got up from behind his desk and walked around. He stood before her, interrupting the beam of light that streamed into the room. Katie felt a sudden coolness on her face and looked up at the clean-shaven counselor.

Hardgrove reached out for the soft hands of the sophomore collegian and drew her to her feet. The two stood only inches from each other.

Katie's wet eyes met those of her mentor. The counselor's hands were warm and reassuring. The aromatic fragrance of his citrus cologne floated in the air filling her senses. It was his scent and she breathed in the sweet vapors. Suddenly, she felt weak. A warm flash made its way up her spine causing dormant hormones to flood the student's body. Katie's cheeks began to burn. There was no sun between them. The heat came from within and she didn't understand the new and strange sensations.

Chapter 5 – Breaking the Ice

"Katie, will you have dinner with me tonight?" Hardgrove asked in a gentle tone. "I would like to get to know you better."

The flush in Katie's cheeks spread rapidly, traveling down her neck and into her bosom. Her breathing quickened and her breasts heaved against the silk blouse that held back her passion.

This isn't right, I can't allow this to happen, she thought to herself as she pulled away from her gallant admirer.

The couple separated their clasped hands, breaking the spark that ignited Katie's desire and the powerful emotions carried with it. She turned away, took a deep breath, allowing the heat within her to cool She turned back again, facing the college professor. This time, her

17

shyness turned into assertion. She measured her words carefully and spoke deliberately, chiding the father figure for his advances.

"Mr. Hardgrove, I don't think this is a good idea…I mean you *are* my counselor!"

Hardgrove immediately recognized his impropriety and the effect it had on his student.

"I'm so sorry. I didn't mean to upset you," he said genuinely. "Katie, I just want to talk…nothing else, I promise. If you like we can go to a public place."

Hardgrove's plea sounded genuine enough, but long standing feelings of guilt continued to plague the lumberman's daughter. She felt the urge to run and hide. Then she recalled Hardgrove's recent words to her: 'Don't you think you are entitled to a life?'

The words rang true to the faithful logger's daughter and instinctively, she knew that changes had to be made. If she were ever to have a life, this was an opportunity.

"Okay," she said, breaking out in a smile while sniffling.

"I'll need to shower and change my clothes. Do you know where I live?"

"I'll find it for sure," Hardgrove answered confidently, his eyes sparkling with joy.

"How about 6 O'clock?"

Katie acknowledged the hour, picked up her knapsack and waved as she walked into the hallway. The afternoon sunlight created a long shadow that narrowed in front of her. Soon she and the shadow were gone and the book-packing student faded from sight.

Chapter 6 – Dinner for Two

The time was 5:45 p.m. Hardgrove was early. He sat outside Katie's small cottage, the motor of his small hybrid automobile idling quietly. Winona Drive sat at the southwestern end of Salem in the community of Mill Creek right off the Willamette River. The street was lined with tall cedars and plush with green shrubs. Small cottages owned mostly by loggers dotted the landscape.

Hardgrove leaned across his steering wheel looking for signs of movement in the small home. A female shadow momentarily darkened one of the white window curtains. The guidance counselor tried to follow the moving target visually but was unable to get a clear view.

Hardgrove checked his watch. It was 5:50 p.m. and the sun was beginning to set. Long autumn rays of sunshine painted the sky with pastel colors as the orange sun gradually descended to the horizon. Suddenly the peaks of the tall cedars were on fire, lit with brilliant streaks of light. Within seconds, the fire was out as the sun's rays climbed down the thick trunks of the giant slow-growing timber.

It was 6 p.m. when Katie opened the front door and looked outside. Hardgrove picked up the sudden movement and waved to the shapely figure standing in wait. Opening his car door, the lanky master of education stepped out and walked briskly toward his dinner date.

Katie's shiny auburn hair was pulled back and up, fastened in place with a tortoise-shell comb. She wore a brown brocade blouse and tan flounced skirt. Around her waist, she wore a wide brown belt with copper eyelets. A pair of tan half-inch heels and gold stud earrings completed her outfit.

Hardgrove greeted Katie enthusiastically, but was careful not to show any affection.

"Wow, you look stunning," he said, standing far enough back for a full body view.

Katie, trying not to show her anxiety, greeted her advisor with a smile.

"Hi, you look nice too," she answered nervously.

The 5-foot 3-inch, 19-year-old college girl was on her first real date and her experienced guidance counselor was well aware of his responsibilities and limitations.

Hardgrove made 6:30 reservations at La Bohème, one of the best French restaurants in Salem. The fine-dining establishment certainly lived up to its reputation for good food, but its choice for the evening was made for a different reason.

Hardgrove opened the door for Katie and approached the restaurant podium. A dark good-looking man in a black tuxedo stood behind the lectern waiting to greet his customers.

"Good evening Frank, nice to see you, how many in your party?"

Overhearing the personal greeting, Katie's eyes widened and her chin dropped ever so slightly.

Claude Guilbert, the restaurant's evening maître d', taught French at Willamette University and was an ex-roommate of Hardgrove. He was married with two children, lived in Salem and worked at La Bohème to supplement his university paycheck.

Knowing Guilbert gave Hardgrove an edge on service at the well-known French restaurant. The best table, the finest wine and the most flamboyant desserts would be at his beckoned call. Hardgrove knew Katie had reservations about going out with him and he had hopes that the dining experience would lesson her anxiety.

Guilbert ushered the couple to a private corner table in the back of the restaurant. The suave maître d' held the chair for Katie as she took her place. He placed a pink linen napkin in her lap, and wished the couple 'bon appétit' before departing.

Katie sipped some water from a crystal glass, admiring the red velour décor that filled the room with plush warm tones. Her eyes were wide with excitement and she smiled broadly. The lumberjack's daughter was humbled yet awed at the extreme lavishness.

"Mr. Hardgrove, this place is amazing," Katie's brown eyes sparkled as she addressed her guidance counselor.

"Katie, please call me Frank. You do realize that we're out on a date?"

"Yes, but I'm so used to calling you Mr. Hardgrove…it sounds funny to call you Frank."

Katie looked into the blue piercing eyes of her therapist and then glanced at the wall in embarrassment. Her small mouth curled up as she licked her lips. She sipped again from the crystal glass before gazing once more into the penetrating orbits.

"Katie, I feel very special with you. I don't know why, but I am really taken in by you. Maybe it's your innocence or your goodness…I'm not sure what it is, but I know that I am feeling something that I haven't felt in a long time."

Katie listened to the words of her counselor and her heart quickened. No one had spoken so lovingly to her before. Suddenly, she was overwrought with emotion. Tears filled her eyes and she dabbed them with her pink napkin.

"Mr. Hardgrove...I mean Frank, I don't know what to say," she said, sobbing slightly. "You are very sweet and I really like you, but this is all very new to me...I mean having a relationship...I know that I am 19, and that by my age, I should have already had...but I'm scared." The words came hard. "And what about my counseling sessions? Will you continue to see me?"

Frank reached across the table and placed his hands on Katie's.

"Katie, you don't have to worry," he said softly. "You're under no obligation. I don't want you to feel like I am pressuring you into something. We'll take it nice and slow and if you don't feel like seeing me again, it's okay. As far as school, I will turn your file over to Annie Miller. She is a psychologist and a great counselor with lots of experience and I know you will get along great with her. Besides, I see where your grades are improving. I think you are getting back on track."

Katie felt Frank's warm hands on hers and the familiar flush of the early afternoon returning. Her heart fluttered and her breasts heaved once again as she struggled to regain her composure.

Frank made everything seem so easy. His explanations were those of an insightful counselor who knew just the right words. But can I trust him? she thought to herself.

Chapter 7 – Opening Moves

Frank ordered a tender pepper-crusted Chateâubriand with broiled tomatoes, thinly sliced scalloped potatoes and butter-logged baby zucchini and patty-pan squash. Katie's choice was the wild, barely cooked salmon with Wasabi pea purée, Fava beans and asparagus, in Yuzu butter. Upon seeing the couple's order, Maître d' Guilbert, sent over two glasses of wine, compliments of the house: red Bordeaux for Frank and a white Pinot Noir for Katie.

Throughout the dinner-wait, Frank and Katie sipped on their wines with Frank refilling the glasses at every opportunity. The alcohol loosened the tongues of the youthful couple and their initial judicious conversation became increasingly unguarded.

"So Frank," Katie asked, slightly slurring her words and giggling. "What's a good looking guy like you doing at Willamette? What brought you out West?"

"I got lucky," Frank answered. "If you want to work at the university level, you normally need a Ph.D. or Ed. D. Willamette was willing to take me on with only a master's degree because of the current shortage of qualified people. I expect that when they find someone with a doctorate, they will probably give me the boot."

"What would you do then?" Katie replied.

"I'd probably have to accept a position at a high school. guidance counselors are very much in demand these days. Kids are pretty mixed up when they get into their teens; many of them need counseling."

"Yeah, like me," Katie giggled.

She picked up her glass and sipped some more of the grape ferment. On her second glass, Katie's cheeks were flushed; her eyes glistened; the room was beginning to spin ever so slowly.

Frank, on the third glass of his Bordeaux, smiled broadly, enjoying Katie's mild intoxication. She was naturally beautiful and he couldn't help but stare at her features. Her oval face complimented her deep brown eyes and long lashes. Freckles dotted the small nose that seemed to be placed perfectly within the symmetrical ellipse. Her full, barely colored lips pursed upward, causing dimples to form every time she smiled.

Frank filled Katie's glass again. She noticed the devilish look on his face as he placed the near empty bottle on the table.

"Frank," she said giggling. "Are you trying to get me drunk so you can take advantage of me?"

Katie raised her eyebrows and tilted her head questioning the counselor's motives. She waited for an answer.

"You know, the way I am feeling right now, I'm afraid to answer you."

Both laughed and drank some more. It took 25 minutes before the heated platters of French cuisine were brought to the table. The waiter, dressed in a formal white shirt with black vest and red bow tie, held the hot entrees with folded linens. He placed the dishes delicately before his guests with a 'hot-don't-touch' warning.

Their palates fully anesthetized with the fruit of the vine, the couple indulged themselves in the presence of a scented candle that glowed and flickered romantically in the red recess of the restaurant.

**

It was after 10 p.m. when Katie noticed the time.

"Frank, we'd better go. I've got an 8 O'clock class."

Frank checked his watch and reacted with disappointment.

"Jeez, I can't believe it's this late. Seems like we just got here."

Frank reached for the black leather wallet with the monogrammed American Express emblem. It had sat on the couple's table unnoticed since the flaming Crêpes Suzette were served an hour before. He checked the bill and noticed the wine charge missing.

I must remember to thank Guilbert, he thought to himself.

Frank left a $100 bill in the wallet before walking Katie to the entrance. He held onto her arm for support as well as affection.

The drive to Mill Creek was made with ease despite the fuzzy heads of the occupants. The couple laughed the whole way home, each recounting their own version of the evening.

Frank turned onto Winona Drive and drove slowly down the dark street waiting for Katie's signal to stop. The hybrid engine hummed its way to the small cottage and quit as Frank turned the key to the off position. He left his keys dangling in the ignition wondering if they would remain there.

"Well, we're here," Frank leaned back in his seat, staring at Katie, his flushed face begging for an invitation. Katie leaned over and kissed the warm cheek gently. Before he could react, the collegian had her hand on the door handle.

"Thank you Frank, I had a wonderful evening. I hope we can do it again," she said, opening the door and stepping outside.

Frank had a different idea. He had his hand on his door when Katie stopped him in his tracks.

"It's okay Frank, I'll see myself in."

The counselor received the message loud and clear. There was no invitation here tonight, not even a hint of one.

Stay cool, he thought to himself. *There will be other opportunities.*

Chapter 8 – What's New

"Hello,"

"Laura, hi – it's me, Katie."

"Katie, gosh, it's been so long. I don't think we've spoken since your father…"

"I know," Katie interrupted, "how are you?"

"Okay, I guess, how about you?"

"I'm so excited, I had to call you."

"What's going on – tell me."

Katie lay prone across her black and white plaid comforter, her bare-feet crossed behind her. Her painted toes wiggled fiercely as she bared her heart to her friend.

"I am seeing somebody," Katie exploded with a giggle.

"What?" Laura questioned in surprise.

"Well, I'm not actually seeing him, but we had a date."

"Who is he? Where did you meet him? Tell me," Laura fired off her questions excitedly.

"He's my guidance counselor..."

"Your what?" Laura interrupted incredulously.

"Yeah, Mr. Hardgrove – he's so handsome. He has beautiful blue eyes and he's really cute."

"Mr. Hardgrove," Laura laughed, "is that what you call him?"

Realizing her faux pas, Katie chuckled.

"Oh gosh, you know, it wasn't till our date was half over that I started calling him by his first name."

"Yeah, and what might that be?"

"Oh, his name is Franklin, but he told me to call him Frank."

Laura listened intently. She knew that Katie hadn't dated and wondered what had changed. She thought about asking, but decided to hold her tongue. She was thrilled to hear the good news and it showed in her voice.

"So, Frank...that's great Katie. Where did you go? What did you do?"

"He took me to this fabulous place downtown. I think it's called La Bohème; a very fancy French restaurant. I drank so much wine that I don't remember much about it. I know it was very expensive and Frank knew the maître d'."

"You bad girl – you got drunk?"

"Well not drunk-drunk, just a little tipsy."

Both girls laughed.

"Laura, you would really like him; he's so gentle and kind."

"I'll bet, not like Sam, I'm sure."

Katie heard the disappointment in her friend's voice and suddenly felt guilty about her joy.

"What's going on with you guys?" Katie asked concerned.

"It isn't good, Katie. I don't know why I stay with him. In the beginning, he was very attentive and I was so impressed with his success and all that, but now it's like he's all caught up with his work; he must work 100 hours a week – or he's doing something else with his time. But, hey…you don't need to hear about that; tell me more. When are you going to see him again?"

"I'll probably see him in school tomorrow. I normally see him every Tuesday afternoon for counseling, but that's not going to happen any more – conflict of interest, you know." Katie said knowingly.

"Did you go to bed with him?" Laura asked openly.

Katie laughed nervously, trying to think of an appropriate response. She felt embarrassed and didn't know how to answer. The two friends had shared everything growing up – everything that is except what happened at home, at night when the lights were out.

Katie stared outside at the golden leaves waving in the sunlight, her eyes fixed in a trance. Laura's personal question brought back memories – unpleasant ones stored deep in her subconscious. She waited while the terrifying dark images completed their script. The ruminations came often. The triggers were everywhere.

"Katie, are you there?" Laura shouted, thinking she'd lost her connection.

The yell shook Katie back to reality. Her eyes came alive and she glanced away from the window, regaining her focus. She repeated Laura's question out loud adding emphasis.

"Did I go to bed with him? Why Laura, now you have me blushing. I just met Frank...it was our first date."

"Oops, sorry, I wasn't thinking...it's just that, well, it's so old-hat to me. I know that you..." Laura caught herself in mid sentence. She didn't want to repeat something cruel. "I mean, you know, it's nice to have those puppy-love feelings. I envy you. I wish I could have that thrill once again." Laura sniffled.

Katie heard the anguish in Laura's voice and felt guilty about going on.

"Laura, we need to get together to talk, to catch up. When can I see you?" Katie asked, feeling empathy for her friend.

"Katie, I would love to catch up with you. I've got a lot to talk about and I could really use your ear."

"Great," Katie replied. "How about next week some time? Let's do lunch together."

"Fine, we'll do it. I want to hear all about Frank," Laura said kindly, holding back her tears.

Chapter 9 – More Counseling

It was Tuesday afternoon and time once again for a counseling session. Katie knocked, then opened the door to the office of Dr. Anne Miller. She looked around and peered inside the inner office. No one was present. She placed her heavy book load on the floor and sat down in the mahogany wingback chair reserved for students.

She visually examined the many diplomas on the wall, reflecting on which certificate she would receive at graduation. Suddenly, the door opened. Frank Hardgrove, the ever-present gentlemen, held the door for Dr. Miller who entered the office first.

"Hi Katie," Hardgrove greeted his former client with an air of unfamiliarity. Anne Miller stood smiling silently as the introduction was made.

"This is Anne Miller," he left off the Dr. "I've just finished briefing her on your case and she's prepared to meet with you and continue your counseling."

Anne Miller moved toward Katie and extended her hand.

Not this again, Katie thought to herself. *I'm going to have to start all over.*

Katie stood properly and greeted the mid-fifties counselor, noticing the rather large diamond ring on her finger. *I guess its Mrs. Miller, or is it Dr. Mrs. Miller*, she thought, feeling a giggle coming on.

"Mr. Hardgrove has told me all about you and I'm sure we are going to get along just fine," Miller suggested. "Why don't we go into my office and talk."

Hardgrove winked at Katie, then excused himself and exited the office. Katie followed Dr. Miller into her office and took a seat by her desk. She looked around the rather dark office with heavy furniture and wondered if there was a light switch. Unlike, Mr. Hardgrove's office, there was no window in the back room and it felt a bit stuffy.

Miller opened the manila file and reviewed Hardgrove's notes. Katie sat silently, her heart beating faster than normal. She nervously tapped her foot on the floor not realizing the signals she was sending out.

The Vanderbilt educated Ph.D. was actually 59-years-old but looked at least ten years younger. She was petite, about 5 feet and wore a size 3 dress. Her hair was bleached blonde and straight. There were no dark roots to reveal her secret. Her makeup although heavy, was blended in nicely and her facial wrinkles were not obvious. She wore a glossy pink lipstick that seemed inappropriate for the senior citizen. Nonetheless, it added a degree of sexiness to the older counselor that couldn't be denied.

Dr. Miller closed her file before looking up and speaking.

"Well Katie, it looks like your grades have come up since you've been seeing Mr. Hardgrove. How do you explain that?"

Katie hesitated before answering. She crossed her legs and straightened her skirt.

"I'm not sure. I guess I'm dealing better."

Miller gave the answer some thought before replying.

"Are you referring to your father's passing?"

Katie stirred nervously as she dodged a fleeting trigger thought.

"Well, yes, I suppose that I am coming to terms with it. I'm concentrating better in class."

"What was your father like?" the skilled counselor asked, noting the deficiency in the file.

"He was a very hard worker and he was very well liked. He was tall and good looking and..."

"Yes, Katie and what? Miller asked, trying to fill in the gap.

"He loved my mother very much." Katie added.

"How do you know that?" Miller asked, looking for a lead. "I mean, your mother died in childbirth almost twenty years ago?"

Katie looked the Ph.D. directly in the eye. Her own eyes began to swell and the familiar blur caused by wet tears made her reach for a tissue. Dr. Miller eased the tissue box closer to the student. The noted psychologist and head of the Guidance Department instinctively knew she had touched a nerve.

"My father was loyal to her. He was never with another woman…and he loved me!"

Katie was now sobbing. The last few words were revealing, almost surreal. The intuitive counselor recognized the inconsistent thought. Her mind rushed to understand the connection.

He loved "me", she said he loved "me," how odd? What's the connection between that and her reference to her father never being with another woman?

Dr. Miller was at a critical point. Pursuing the line of questioning might create an impasse or breakdown in their communication.

I could lose her altogether, she thought to herself. *I need more time to gain her trust; time for further exploration.* She switched the subject.

"Katie, I didn't mean to upset you. Why don't we talk about something more pleasant?"

"I'm okay," Katie dabbed her eyes. "It's just that when I'm reminded of my father, I get emotional."

"I understand," Miller replied. "We'll come back to your father later on."

"I see by your file that you've had eight sessions with Mr. Hardgrove. Did the two of you get along?"

"Very well – Frank, I mean Mr. Hardgrove was always very nice and he's been very helpful."

The Ph.D. heard Katie's informality and wondered if she had uncovered an unethical breach of practice.

"Tell me more about Mr. Hardgrove, she followed up," probing her hidden suspicion.

"Gee, I don't know what to say. I guess he told you that we were dating, I mean…we had a date."

Anne Miller sat back in the swivel chair, which creaked every time she moved. Her eyebrows raised every so slightly and her forehead makeup cracked from the furrows that suddenly appeared in her brow.

"Hmm," she replied, trying to act nonchalant. Hardgrove had kept his impropriety from her. *Another breach of ethics,* she thought to herself. When transferring the case to her, he pretended to have a scheduling conflict.

What do I do now? she thought, *dating your student and withholding the relationship is forbidden by the rules. I don't have a choice. I will have to file an incident report. At least he had sense enough to transfer the case.*

Dr. Miller checked her watch. Her time with Katie was almost up; she had another student waiting on the mahogany chair.

"Katie, we got a late start today; why don't we continue this next Tuesday?"

Katie rose from her chair and straightened her skirt. Before departing, she turned to Dr. Miller.

"I hope I didn't get Mr. Hardgrove in trouble," she said, wiping the remnants of her tears. "I guess he didn't tell you."

Dr. Miller came around from her desk and escorted Katie to the door.

"Don't worry about it dear, it won't go any further," she lied.

Chapter 10 – A Second Date

In 1942, a star grove of five sequoia redwoods was planted on the campus grounds to celebrate the 100th anniversary of the founding of Willamette University. The magnificent grove became a favorite spot for students to congregate.

Katie sat at the base of a giant sequoia sucking the remaining juices from a Macintosh apple core. As she tasted the last vestiges of her fruit, she read from "Life in the Siuslaw Valley," a historical book about Kalupuya, Siuslaw and Yoncalla Indians.

Frank Hardgrove made his appearance without notice.

"Hi, anything interesting? the counselor asked, his hands in his pockets.

Katie surprised by the intrusion, looked up at the handsome six-footer and recognized him immediately. He seemed even taller from her perspective.

"Hi," she said, wondering how he happened to find her. "I'm taking my lunch break."

"I know," Hardgrove replied. "I just left Anne Miller. She told me she saw you at the grove."

"Mrs. Miller – what were you doing with her, checking up on me?" Katie asked, smiling.

"That wouldn't be ethical without your consent, but I did tell her that I was seeing you. I hesitated telling her the other day because of the school rules, but I thought about it and decided that it was better that I be truthful with her."

"Well, she already knew. I told her about you on Tuesday. I didn't know…"

"It's okay, she knows that I am violating school rules, but I think she's cool with it. Annie is pretty hip; she's up there in years but you'd never know it from the way she dresses and handles herself."

Katie put her book to the side and watched Hardgrove lower himself to the grassy plot, taking his place beside her. He wore a tweed sports jacket, an open necked white oxford shirt and blue jeans that hugged his body in all the right places.

Katie sat smiling, happy to see her former counselor. She remembered her first date with him two weeks before.

What a wonderful evening, she thought.

She hadn't heard from him since that momentous evening and wondered if there would ever be a second date.

Hardgrove grabbed the hard cover book and thumbed through the pages.

"Still with the Indians, huh. Seen any lately?" he joked.

"I see them all the time," Katie replied, "they just don't dress that way any more."

"Oh, you mean they don't wear those feather headdresses to school?" he replied sarcastically.

Katie chuckled and suddenly there was silence. He was doing it again. He was staring at her with those deep blue gorgeous eyes. She felt the blood rushing through her 110-pound body, her cheeks warmed by the sudden flow. Those strange sensations, which she didn't understand, once again filled her with desire. She tried desperately to control the flush.

It must be so obvious, she thought.

"You're staring at me," Katie said sheepishly, embarrassed by her evident color. "Why do you do that?"

Hardgrove moved closer. She could smell the familiar citrus cologne that filled her senses on their first date.

"I'm just looking at your beautiful face," he replied, reaching for her hand. "I only have a few minutes. My next appointment is at 1 p.m. Can I see you this weekend?"

Katie felt the warmth of the male hand on hers and her heart quickened at the question.

"Sure, call me – you have my number."

"Okay, I'll call you tonight and we'll set something up, Hardgrove answered hurriedly."

The counselor released his grip on Katie's hand and rose to his feet.

"There's a jazz concert at the outdoor amphitheater Saturday evening. Maybe we could take in the show?" he said, turning towards the school. "I've never been there but I understand it's quite a place."

"Sounds like fun," Katie replied. "You'll still call me? Katie questioned insecurely"

Hardgrove nodded and made his way quickly up the main path. Katie watched her new boyfriend's figure grow smaller as he approached the university entrance in the distance.

She looked up at the blue cloudless canopy, framed by a five-star formation of gold autumn leaves, day-dreaming about her forthcoming date.

He must like me – he's asking me out again, she thought. *But should I be happy or scared?*

Chapter 11 – Jazz It Up

The Salem outdoor amphitheater was built on an old quarry site on the north side of town. Twenty tiers of crescent shaped concrete pads, serve as seating for the 1,500-person arena. A huge 4,000 square-foot stage with rising orchestra pit completes the entertainment setting.

The September evening was cool – around 63 degrees, with a slight breeze that carried the scent of lilacs growing in the fields above the quarry. A clear starry sky presented the perfect backdrop for listening to the smooth sounds of jazz, presented by up and coming musicians, seeking a name.

Katie and Frank sat in the two end seats of row I, about 40 feet from the stage. With the stadium-type seating and the crescent shaped arena, there wasn't a bad seat in the house, especially at concerts, where Surround Sound made every seat a listening booth.

Outdoor events in Salem called for casual dress. In September when the evening temperatures dropped into the 60's, most patrons wore sweaters or light jackets.

Katie, dressed in black slacks and a three-quarter-sleeve white knit jersey top, carried a black cotton sweater trimmed with pink roses. Frank wore his traditional blue jeans and sport coat.

The couple took their seats at 7:45 p.m., fifteen minutes before show time. Frank, sitting at the end of the row, rubbed his hands briskly trying to ward off the slight chill he felt coming on. Katie, wedged in between Frank and an elderly woman, had more body heat protecting her, but donned her sweater anyway. This was an exciting evening for Frank and Katie. Neither had been to the amphitheater before. Frank impressed by the rugged architecture, expressed his thoughts out loud.

"This place is awesome – what a great idea to build an outdoor concert hall here. I understand they once mined gold and silver under our seats."

Katie followed Frank's eyes but was taken in more by the people than the rocky surroundings. It was a full house and everyone was busily chatting and buying drinks from the roving vendors. Katie reviewed the playbill reading about the scheduled entertainment, when she felt Frank's arm around her shoulder. The pupils of her brown eyes dilated and her heart quickened in response to the affectionate gesture but she continued to read, visibly composed and unperturbed.

"Oh look, Frank," Katie observed a familiar name on the playbill. "Josh McCreary, I think I know this guy. If it's the same one, he plays the organ at our church."

Frank peered over Katie's shoulder pulling her closer as he reviewed the playbill. The scent of jasmine filled his nostrils and he knew the chemistry was right.

How will this evening end, he thought to himself. *Can I be a gentleman around her, controlling my desire, or should I throw caution to the wind and indulge my fantasies?*

**

Philip Sullivan, the master of ceremonies and amphitheater director stood at the foot of the stage adjusting the microphone. He tested the sound system by tapping on the black receiver looking for a nod of approval from the sound technician.

Suddenly, a piano, four music stands and chairs magically appeared on stage. Lights illuminated the theatre while two spotlights danced around the rostrum. The director took the microphone from its platform and waited for the audience's attention.

"Ladies and gentlemen, welcome to this special evening's jazz performance," he said, looking out into the crowded seats. The audience responded with applause and some inappropriate hooting.

"Thank you. You are in for a real treat tonight as the Salem Amphitheater brings you some new and special talent in the music industry. This one-night concert features local jazz groups from the Salem area as well as a touring group from Sydney, Australia. There will be one fifteen-minute intermission at 9 p.m. It now gives me great pleasure to introduce our first jazz group from Mill Creek. Please give it up for the *Rivermen*."

A wave of applause filled the quarry in response to the city's well-known jazz group. The *Rivermen* performed nightly at *Center City*, a high-end nightclub frequented by the professional elite.

Five neatly dressed musicians in sparkling black tuxedos took their positions on stage. Four sat behind silver mirrored bandstands, embroidered with dark interlocked "C's.' The fifth, Josh McCreary, took his place behind the open ebony Steinway piano.

Katie's eyes strained as the jazz band made their appearance.

"It's him," she shouted excitedly. "It's Josh from our church. I can't believe it. I didn't know he played in a band."

Frank watched Katie's face light up. Her smile hid the pain she felt deep inside and he was glad to share her joy. Being with Frank and spending the night listening to smooth sounds was a perfect diversion for the sophomore on scholastic probation.

The *Rivermen* – Josh McCreary on piano, Robert Sizemore on sax and trumpet, William Barrett on bass,

Arnold French on guitar and Sonny Marone on drums, played Duke Ellington – Count Basie style swing music. Their first selection was *It Don't Mean A Thing If It Ain't Got That Swing*, a song made popular by Duke Ellington in the 30's.

The four beats per measure music put everyone in the mood for an evening of jazz music from the 30's up through modern times. Within seconds, the entire audience was clapping to the rhythm; some brave souls jitterbugged in the aisles.

Frank removed his arm from Katie's shoulder and joined in with the clapping. Katie, caught up in the mood, climbed to her feet and rocked in time to the melodious classic.

The intermission seemed to come in an instant and there was a rush to the public restrooms. As usual, the women's queue was three times as long as the men's. When Katie returned to her seat, Frank was there to greet her.

"Hi, you just made it…the concert is about to begin, are you cold?" he asked, rubbing his hands.

Katie leaned into Frank's open jacket, which he quickly wrapped around her. She felt the warmth of his body and it felt good in the cool night air.

The evening wore on with each group outdoing its predecessor. The touring group from Australia known as the *Aussie Roos* completed the evening with renditions of jazz and blues favorites from the land down under. They played for half an hour, took their bows and played two final songs after being coaxed by a standing ovation.

Frank and Katie walked briskly to the car, humming songs from the concert and skipping to the beats. The guidance counselor held Katie close, his sports jacket surrounding her svelte shivering body. Neither had anything alcoholic, but both were high on jazz.

Conversation was limited on the drive home with Frank doing most of it. Katie was busy focusing on how to handle the good night kiss. She wanted to feel the passion again but she didn't trust herself nor did she trust her date. The confusion stirred up unpleasant memories and guilt and she suddenly felt anxious.

Suppose I kiss him and it leads to more, she thought. *How can I control it? What should I do?*

Frank drove his small car down Winona Drive and pulled up in front of the small cottage, which was now a familiar landmark. As before, he turned off the engine and left the keys hanging in the ignition. He remembered his last date and how abruptly it ended. His mind instructed not to push the envelope but his emotions signaled otherwise.

I wonder if she will invite me in? I really want her. I don't want to hurt her, but I want her to know how much I care. Why are these things always so difficult for me?

The pair sat silently in their front bucket seats separated by a molded gearbox.

I wish I could afford a Goddamned regular car, he cursed to himself. *I can't even reach to put my arm around her, no less kiss her.*

The frustrated counselor sat a moment thinking what to do, before taking the initiative.

"I'll get the door for you," Frank said, quickly opening his door, hoping Katie would wait for him.

He was on the other side in a flash, gripping the door handle. The door squeaked, breaking the silence in the quiet neighborhood. Katie stepped out feeling the need to run to the safety of her house. She hesitated, then turned to face him. In that split second, Frank took advantage of her delay. He put his mouth to her's and kissed her passionately. Katie, surprised by the sudden movement reacted by pulling away, but not before the heat of the kiss made itself known to her innermost desire. She shivered in the coolness of the night and wanted to feel the warmth once again. She looked at the piercing blue eyes that were only inches from her face. She saw the reflection of the moon dancing in the wetness of his eyes and felt drawn to the warm face that hovered over her.

Frank received the signal and kissed her again. Her big brown eyes fluttered before closing tightly. Her arms found the back of his neck and she held him closely allowing his warm lips to touch hers again and again. A mixture of citrus cologne and jasmine oil vapors filled the space between the two faces. The aphrodisiacs only intensified the feelings. Frank felt he was initiating Katie and suddenly felt guilty. His passion was building and he knew where things were headed. He had to stop before he lost control.

"Katie, we can't," he said pulling away. Katie was confused. The warm caress and the softness of his warm lips were new and wonderful. They made her feel like a woman – wanted and desired, for herself and not for perverted sex.

"What's wrong Frank," she cried. "Did I do something...?"

"No, you didn't do anything wrong sweetheart. I'm just scared. I know that I'm not supposed to know, but I do. I know that this is all new for you. I want to take it slow. I don't want to take advantage. We have plenty of time...believe me, another five minutes and we wouldn't be standing here."

Katie looked into the captivating blue eyes and tears rolled down her cheeks.

"Frank, you are so kind and considerate. I have never met anyone like you. I think I'm falling for you."

Frank held Katie in his arms knowing he had done the right thing.

Chapter 12 – Flashback

Jack Cole buried his head into the pillow, his arm around his daughter. The father and daughter had slept together since her birth. As soon as she could talk, he swore her to silence. No one was to know, not even her best friend, Laura Sunshine.

Throughout her early childhood, the sleeping arrangement was innocent enough with her father simply occupying one side of the bed. Katie, not knowing any different, accepted the idea without question. In fact, she liked having him there. It was comforting to have her Daddy at her side.

When she was 14, the incestuous prelude progressed. One night, she felt her father's hand on her small breast. She ignored the gesture, thinking it was an accidental touch. When the perversions continued however, Katie did not react. She would lay frozen, silent with fear, allowing her father to grope and fondle her. After a time, she began accepting the exploits as a natural part of her sleeping routine. In her mind she rationalized the acts as expressions of love and endearment.

She was 16 when he had intercourse with her. It happened in the middle of the night. She awoke, finding her father on top of her.

At first, I thought I was dreaming. It happened so quickly. He rolled over and went to sleep like nothing happened. This occurred again and again. It was then that I realized what sex was all about - at least I thought I did.

Daddy had sex with me until shortly before his accident. In a way it was flattering. But I became confused. I felt more like a wife than a daughter. I knew that our relationship was not normal, but there was nothing I could do. I really hated it but Daddy expected it of me and I always tried to please him. One night, I remember him approaching me. He had been drinking and he reeked from alcohol. I didn't want to have sex with him, but he was insistent. I tried to resist him and he hit me in the face. It hurt so much. I didn't understand why he hit me. He forced himself on me. In the morning, he said he was sorry, but I was angry and began hating him. I promised myself I would never allow him to do that to me again.

I had never seen him drunk before. I don't know why or what started it. Maybe it was something on the job. He never told me. During those last few months, he would come to bed drunk and pass out. I didn't care - at least he didn't bother me. The night before his accident, he had been drinking heavily. I swear, I think that's what killed him. When you're moving around on those logs, you have to be alert and on your toes. He probably went to work drunk. The more I think about it that's probably what happened.

When Daddy died, I was heartsick but I was also relieved; I no longer had to worry about his sexual assaults. But, I was lonely. I missed having him around and I missed his love.

Chapter 13 – Guidance Department

Anne Miller, head of the Guidance Department, called her monthly counselor's meeting to order. Each counselor would discuss the cases they were assigned, updating the director as to the standing, progress and problems of each student. Like a law firm discussing its clients, the university's Guidance Department was run like a business, with work schedules, status reports and evaluations. The only exception was that for privacy purposes, the real names of the students were masked. Anne Miller started the meeting by discussing her cases.

"Case M315 is a 2nd year male student, majoring in biology," she began. "He was sent to the Guidance Department after a cheating incident in his chemistry class. The student carried a 3.8 GPA, prior to the incident. I have seen him three times. During his last visit, he admitted to the cheating, but blamed his fraternity. According to his story, they forced him to provide answers to a failing upperclassman under threat of expulsion. The dean is investigating the incident.

"Case M316 is a second year female student who is on scholarship. She recently lost her father in a mill accident and her grades have been suffering. The student is exhibiting signs of family abuse and needs to be closely monitored."

Anne Miller removed her reading glasses and placed them on the conference table. She closed the file on M316 and spoke to her contemporaries in a stern voice.

"Before I go on," she hesitated. "I have a serious situation, which needs to be addressed. Without mentioning any names," she looked around the table giving each counselor an equal split-second stare. "One of you has broken the university's rule of professional ethics. This same person has also broken the university's rule regarding teacher-student relationships. You know who you are and I won't portend to embarrass you by mentioning your name in this forum.

"It is important for each of us to remember that we, above all other personnel in this university, are charged with ethical standards that are in place because of the sensitivity of our positions. What we do and the way we interact with our students impacts their lives, not only in an academic way, which is certainly central to their goals at the university, but more importantly, their emotional lives. Because of our unique position, we must guard against any breach of our ethical standards. To those of you who may have misjudged my appreciation for enforcing these rules, I say to you, look again. Do not be fooled by my dress, my physical appearance or my demeanor. I take my position as head of this department in the most serious vain and I expect each of you to follow suit."

Frank Hardgrove squirmed in his seat listening to the tongue-lashing. Miller's demeanor and dress had indeed fooled him into complacency. Equating her chic appearance with indifference to the rules was a big mistake and his realization came about much too late.

Frank pondered whether his colleagues were aware of his relationship with Katie and understood that Miller's comments were directed at him.

Anne Miller completed her report while Frank sat quietly engrossed in his own thoughts. It was hard for him to concentrate once Miller disclosed that Katie had been abused. Case M316 was certainly Katie; he was sure of it. The thought of her being abused turned the blue-eyed educator's stomach. Everything was coming into focus.

He pondered the words of his director, Anne Miller, Anne Miller, Ph.D. that is, and he knew she was right. It was wrong for him to be involved with a student and especially one that was his therapy client. But, it was too late for regrets and impossible to turn his feelings around. Frank's mind was made up; he would continue to see Katie, despite the serious warning but he would be compassionate and kind. She needed his understanding and real love. He would provide both.

Chapter 14 – Double Trouble

Frank Hardgrove spoke in a hushed voice to the party on the other end of the phone. His chair was turned to the window when Katie entered his office.

"Yes, I know," he said unaware of her presence. "I'm scared George. I think a pink slip is on the way. I really need your help. Can you check it out for me?" There was a pause and then Frank's reply. "Okay, I'll look to hear from you the first of the week."

Frank pulled the tangled phone cord from around his chair and hung up the phone. He turned around and was startled to see Katie standing at his desk.

"Well, surprise...what are you doing here?" Frank stood up and greeted Katie with a brief hug and kiss.

"Is everything okay? Katie retorted. "What's this about a pink slip?" she asked.

"How are you? I was just thinking about you." Frank answered, bypassing the question.

"Sit down," he gestured with his outstretched arm.

Katie continued standing, defying his invitation.

"You didn't answer my question, Frank. Why have you been avoiding me? I haven't heard from you all week."

Frank pursed his lips tightly and sighed. *Should I tell her about the meeting?* he questioned silently.

"Katie, I've had a lot on my mind this week."

"What is it Frank? Is something wrong? Did I do something...?

Katie stopped in the middle of her sentence. Her large brown eyes suddenly glistened with tears as undeserved guilt overcame her.

"No Katie," he answered, "you didn't do anything. It's just...well sit down and let me explain."

Frank closed the door to his office and once again invited Katie to sit down. This time she obliged.

"Katie, the other day at our department meeting, I was admonished for having a personal relationship with you. I didn't think that Annie, I mean Dr. Miller would have cared a hoot, but obviously I was wrong. She reamed me out good, accusing me of breaking all of the university rules and contributing to your emotional upheaval. I was embarrassed in front of my colleagues and to be honest with you, I think I am going to be facing a disciplinary hearing or worse. It doesn't look good."

Katie listened intently wondering where the explanation was headed. *Is he going to dump me?* she thought, fearing the worst.

The tears came even faster and the feelings of guilt that were her normal companion became overwhelming. Katie wept openly, sobbing in between the gasps for air. Frank reached across his desk and held Katie's hands tightly.

"Katie, for God's sake, stop crying," he barked at her.

"Nothing is going to change between us. I love you!"

He hesitated realizing the magnitude of his words. He had never uttered those sacred words to anyone other than his mother.

I can't believe I said it, he thought to himself.

The three words meant a lot to the educator, but they meant even more to Katie.

"I love you too, Frank," she said whimpering. "I'm so sorry, I never meant to get you into trouble. What are we going to do?"

"We're going to keep seeing each other," Frank said sternly. "If I get canned, we're still going to see each other. I see a future for you and me, Katie. I'm not going to throw that away."

There was silence and then the embrace. Frank rose from his chair, never releasing his grasp on the two clammy hands clutched in his own. He kissed Katie warmly on the lips, tasting the salty tears that covered her face. Katie broke the clasp and placed her arms around the 24-year-old guidance counselor, pressing her mouth into his. He held her tightly, warmly, reassuringly.

The silhouette of the two embraced lovers revealed itself as a shadow in the opaque door window. Like the signal for Batman over the skies of Gotham City, the message sent out was clear to all that took notice.

Dr. Anne Miller, the only one that really mattered, was the first and last to see the revealing image. Her fateful path by Frank Hardgrove's office during the interlude was an incredible coincidence, which sealed the fate of her co-worker and friend. She recognized the cast inside the counselor's office and knew her duty as well.

Chapter 15 – A Surprise

Katie placed the phone down on its cradle. It was 11 p.m. and the sophomore Willamette student was in bed, buried beneath her soft checkered quilt. She and Frank had talked for over an hour. The calls came regularly since their last meeting. Frank seemed determined to move forward with their relationship. Much of their conversation dealt with talk about a future together. Katie delighted in the loving words of affection bestowed upon her. It comforted her loneliness and helped with her depression.

**

It was Friday evening and Frank drove his hybrid towards the small cottage on Winona Drive in Mill

Creek. Officially, this was the third date for the couple and both were apprehensive; Katie, because she knew about third dates and the expectations, and Frank because of his newly gained knowledge about her abuse. The obligations and consequences of intimacy prayed heavily on the mind of the educator as he approached the address of his rendezvous.

Katie slipped on her jeans and checked herself out in the bureau mirror. She stepped back and made a half turn, looking back at her bottom. The fit was good. Her small well-rounded butt filled the denims in made-to order-fashion.

Outside, Frank sat in the small semi-electric automobile, the engine purring. He turned off the ignition and peered into the lit windows of the bungalow, looking for any signs of life. He squinted hard, then noticed the familiar small figure prancing back and forth between the bedroom and living room.

Frank tapped slightly on his horn. The tinny sound echoed through the quiet neighborhood. Katie came to the front window and signaled with a wave of her hand. The lights in the small cottage suddenly went dark and Katie walked out, closing the door behind her.

Frank was on the other side of the car with the door partially opened. Katie approached with a big smile, her teeth glistening in the night. The pair embraced before entering the small sedan.

"Hi, how are you?" Katie asked, still smiling.

"Fine, you look great," he answered, returning the smile.

"Thanks, so what are we doing?"

"I told you it was going to be a surprise," Frank replied.

"When are you going to tell me?"

"I'm not…just going to surprise you," he answered with a sheepish grin.

"Okay," she said, "let's go."

Frank started the engine and made a quick U-turn. He drove up Winona Drive following the signs to the Salem turnpike. A few miles down the highway, Frank exited east onto Route 22.

"I have no idea where we're going," Katie laughed. "Are you planning to kidnap me?" she asked, looking out the window.

Frank reached across the gearbox and patted Katie on her knee, reassuring her. They were outside the city limits and except for the headlights of the road, there was darkness everywhere. The sky was clear and stars filled the vastness. A quarter moon was visible in the distant horizon.

They drove for almost an hour before Frank turned off at Exit I-5. A green and white exit sign read *Detroit Lake Campgrounds*. Recognizing the sign, Katie's mouth opened in surprise.

"Detroit Lake," she cried out excitedly. "Frank, is this the surprise?"

"Wait," he replied, "you haven't seen anything yet."

The little hybrid climbed up the winding road, its engine whining and downshifting automatically. At the top of the road, Frank pulled into a clearing overlooking a 3,500-acre lake.

The U.S. Army Corps of Engineers constructed the man-made body of water in 1951 and named it Detroit Lake. The property, located in the Cascade Mountains below Mt. Jefferson, is part of the Willamette Forest.

Frank opened the door for Katie and she stepped out gingerly, watching her footsteps. The crescent moon's reflection shimmered off the huge reservoir of water. Katie held Frank's hand as they walked closer to the water's edge.

"This is so beautiful," Katie said, squeezing Frank's hand. "I'm glad you didn't tell me.

Katie looked up at the clear starry canopy and pointed in the direction of a streak of light that quickly disappeared.

"Look, a shooting star," she said, thrilled at the sight. "This is so romantic."

"I thought you'd like it," Frank said, hugging Katie.

"The sign...it said *campgrounds.* Where do people stay?"

"Some camp out in tents or trailers, others rent cabins or stay at the inn."

"Oh yeah," Katie laughed devilishly.

Recognizing the mischievous tone of her voice, Frank followed up.

"Would you like to see the accommodations?"

"What's that?" she responded, taking more time to consider the invitation.

"Nothing, I was just talking to myself. It's just so beautiful out here." Frank reigned in his desire.

"You said something about an inn? Katie inquired again?"

"I did, but we don't have to…"

"I'd love to see it," she answered quickly, interrupting his sentence. Frank squeezed Katie and the two embraced.

Frank wanted more intimacy with Katie, but he was apprehensive. He knew that Katie was troubled and that becoming involved sexually might complicate their relationship. Still, he wanted her.

Chapter 16 – Intimacy

The small blue sedan hummed its way over to the camping area following the painted florescent signs that marked the path.

The outline of tents dotted the wooded terrain that encircled the main road. A sign pointing to the inn and cabins was securely mounted on a telephone pole. Frank followed the signs until the road ended in a circle. At the center was a rustic looking two-story mansion. The Lake Inn was built in the 60's to accommodate guests whose lifestyle required a bed and breakfast type establishment. The inn was a great alternative to those who didn't feel comfortable roughing it in the woods.

Frank parked the car on a small gravel lot adjacent to the residence. The couple walked to the front entrance and climbed the thirteen wooden steps to the terrace. At the top, a clear view of the lake and the mountains surrounding it was clearly visible. The snow-covered peak of Mt. Jefferson, at 10,497 feet and the tallest mountain in the Cascades, stood majestically tall against the starry blue background.

Frank and Katie leaned against the porch railing admiring the scenic view. It was close to 9 p.m. A cool breeze made its way down the mountain and across the lake carrying the spicy scent of lavender from surrounding fields. The plant with the lilac blue flower, raised for commercial use of the fragrance, permeated the valley.

Katie inhaled the breeze allowing the healing incense to linger in her breast. The lavender, used for aromatherapy oils, sent waves of tranquility through her 110-pound body. She exhaled and felt the muscles of her neck loosen in response. The tension she felt at the beginning of the evening was gone. She held Frank's arm against her side, feeling his warmth. Frank whispered something in her ear. Katie chuckled.

"Let's go in," she said, "it's getting chilly."

The inn had a grand room with two staircases. A blazing fireplace provided a warm glow to the area. A mahogany counter stood at the far center of the room. Plaques with various credit card emblems sat on its polished surface. An elderly woman stood behind the ledge.

"May I help you?" she asked, anticipating the normal reply.

"Yes," Frank answered. "Do you have any rooms available for this evening?"

The elderly woman paused, giving the couple the once-over. Katie felt the woman's eyes on her and her cheeks began to blush.

"Why yes, we have the Jefferson and Salem rooms available. The Jefferson faces the lake and rents for $150 per night; the Salem faces the woods and rents for $125. The rate includes a full breakfast in our dining room."

Frank looked at Katie for a decision.

"You pick," she said shyly.

"We'll take the Jefferson room," Frank answered, smiling at the octogenarian.

The clerk smiled back, winking at Frank in a rude manner of meaning. She grabbed a key from one of the compartments of the old Wooton desk behind her and handed it to Frank.

"It's up the stairs on the left. Would you like to pay by cash or credit card?"

"Always formalities," he uttered as he reached for his wallet.

**

The Jefferson room was an unimpressive chamber with a small window facing the lake. Frank looked around and wondered if it was worth the extra $25. Katie walked into the tiny bath and flicked on the light.

"How charming," she commented.

"Look out here, the view is great," Frank said sarcastically.

Katie walked to the other side of the room and looked through the small window, almost entirely blocked by a giant sequoia. She laughed as she glimpsed the briefest reflection of the lake between the branches of the huge tree.

"Who cares," she said, gesturing with her arms in the air. "We're here, together and that's all that matters."

Katie placed her arms around Frank. She hugged him tightly, her head resting against his chest. Frank responded wrapping his arms around the college sophomore, pulling her close.

"You feel so good," Frank said, feeling the warmth of the small body against his.

"Hmmm," she sighed, trying to burrow further into the warm chest that heaved with every breath.

Frank pulled Katie from him and looked deeply into her brown eyes.

Her eyes were glistening and inviting. Her cheeks were flushed and her lips were slightly parted. Frank felt the power of her desire. He kissed her, knowing there was no turning back. The two risk takers were prepared to give themselves to one another. The kisses intensified and the couple's passion quickly turned to lust.

Frank carried Katie to the four-poster bed and gently placed her on the down filled quilt. He kissed her passionately – first on her mouth, then on her neck. Katie responded with her own passion. Her desire to be had by her lover intensified. Her sense of reality began to dim as her hormones drove her over the edge.

In a matter of minutes, the two lovers were naked, entwined in a loving embrace. Frank's desire led him on. He guided himself to her, forming a union of love. They were one, and suddenly passion gave way to release. The blue-eyed counselor's world exploded.

Katie was in a different world. Her passion was real but suddenly the image of her father erupted. He was on top of her, his stinking alcoholic breath in her face. His sweat soaked the sheets while he satisfied himself.

"No Daddy, get off of me," she cried out in pain. "I hate you – get the hell off of me." She beat Frank with her fists, pushing at his shoulders, crying hysterically.

Frank rolled off to the side trying to come to grips with the fiction of the moment. He held Katie, trying to comfort her, speaking softly and stroking her hair, which was wet with perspiration.

The trained counselor, shocked by the tirade, tried valiantly to understand the episode.

She was having a psychotic episode, a terrifying flashback. Obviously, her reference to Daddy, was her recently deceased father, Jack Cole – the lumberjack. It all makes sense now. Anne Miller's comments about abuse; it was her incestuous relationship with her father that left her psychologically scarred.

I should have known better. How could I've been so stupid? I don't deserve to be a guidance counselor – look what I have done!

Chapter 17 – The Aftermath

It took Katie a good hour to compose herself. Frank took his time, talking her back to reality. Like a child's night terror, it was difficult convincing her that her perceptions were hallucinatory and that she was safe with him.

When she'd recovered enough to think clearly, Frank helped her dress.

"I don't know what happened to me. All of a sudden I was in a different place – in bed with my father," Katie sobbed.

"It's okay," Frank empathized. "It's over now and you're going to be alright."

Katie's disturbed reaction to their sexual encounter was both frightening and disconcerting to Frank.

Although he seemed completely composed and spoke reassuringly to Katie, his gut told him differently. The episode evoked internal fears of a life strewn with problems. He knew well of mental illness, not only from his classes in psychology, but from a personal standpoint as well. His sister, Belle, spent nine years in a state mental hospital in Roanoke. She was a victim of schizophrenia, a disease, which ultimately left her homeless and a ward of the state.

Frank's exposure to Katie's emotional problems was limited. Until Anne Miller mentioned the abuse thing, he was completely unaware. Even then, he didn't realize the extent of the emotional damage.

Suddenly, He realized that his relationship with Katie was in jeopardy. The internal fears multiplied.

How am I going to deal with this? Do I really want to be thinking about a future with her? What kind of a life would it be? Will she wind up in a mental hospital like Belle?

Frank explored all the 'what ifs' in his mind. He dressed quickly, silently, his thoughts rambling. The strain showed on his face. Katie watched her lover dress and felt his anxiety.

"What are we going to do?" she asked.

"I think I should take you home," Frank answered tying his shoelace.

"Frank, I'm really sorry...I didn't mean to hurt you. It won't happen again, I promise," she pleaded.

"Katie, it's not your fault, but I think you need some rest. I'm very concerned," Frank's fears began to take hold.

Katie's eyes filled with tears, as she stood prepared to follow Frank out the door. He flicked the light switch and led Katie to the staircase, holding her by the elbow.

It was almost 11 p.m. when the couple walked into the grand room past the old women who guarded the front desk. The night clerk looked up, surprised to see the young couple leaving so soon. She inspected the clock on the wall and shook her head in disbelief. The next expression came with a smirk. She thought she knew, but she didn't.

The couple walked rapidly to the front entrance. Katie felt Frank's embarrassment as he hurried her down the steep stairs of the rustic structure and unto the parking lot. The sounds of two car doors opening and closing echoed through the mountainous recreation area. Silence reigned as the couple made their way to the highway.

The ride home seemed extra long without the intimate conversation that absorbed the couple on the way out. There was tension in the air as both passengers clung to their thoughts. The questions and doubts of a future were there but no one dared to express them. Once again, Katie felt guilty and ashamed – just as she had so many times before.

Chapter 18 – Moving On

It was early Monday in Salem, only 9 a.m., and Frank had just settled into his day when the phone call came in.

"Hi George, how are you? I've been waiting to hear from you..." Frank sat back in his swivel chair facing the window.

"You're kidding! Arlington High? Sure I remember Dudley. He's still the principal...? Yeah, I'll bet he did remember me. I spent more than a few hours in his office. What are they looking for? What's the deal?"

Frank placed his right foot on the windowsill and stared out the window, listening to the details of a new position back East.

George Secouris, his old roommate at UVA and high school buddy, spoke intermittently as he munched on his lunch, 3,000 miles away.

"Hmm, sounds interesting. What are they paying?" Frank paused, waiting to hear the important figure.

"You're kidding. That sounds super. I'll mail him my resume today. I hope he doesn't remember too much about us," Frank joked.

There was a pause and then laughter on both ends. Frank reminisced with his old school chum, exchanging stories of devilish pranks engaged in at Arlington High. It was almost 9:30 a.m. when the call ended.

Frank immediately searched his desk drawers for a copy of his resume. He pulled out the single typewritten sheet from a manila file and held it up to the light. Scanning the text, he realized that it was not current. He placed the paper on top of his desk for later editing.

**

Anne Miller entered Hardgrove's office without announcing herself. The guidance counselor was hunched over his desk, entering some notes in a green spiral calendar when her presence interrupted his task. She stood at the foot of his desk and waited for the counselor's attention. She inadvertently spotted the resume on the top of his desk and weighed the irony.

She was about to give Hardgrove his two-week notice; yet, it seemed he already knew. Hardgrove, feeling the presence of another person's stare, looked up from his crouched writing position.

"Well, surprise," he said, smiling and sitting up. Anne Miller immediately felt the gaze of those penetrating blue eyes that sent female hormones raging.

Not today, she thought; *not with me, Buster.*

"Frank, I'm sorry," Anne blurted the words out nervously. This was a first for the tenured psychologist and head of the department. She was visibly upset.

"We're letting you go," she said, her voice dry and waning. She revealed a white envelope from behind her back and placed it gently on top of Frank's resume. The name, Frank Hardgrove was neatly typed on the outside of the envelope. The return address was that of Charles Witter, Chancellor of Willamette.

Frank struggled with the seal of the envelope, finally tearing at it. Inside was the notorious pink sheet, outlining the university's procedure for termination. The counselor laughed nervously, trying to cover up his embarrassment. He'd never been fired before and the drama of the event evoked feelings of guilt and trepidation. He knew why he was being fired. It was obvious from Anne Miller's lecture at the monthly department meeting. Still, he was unprepared. He hadn't moved fast enough securing another job. His options to maintain his reputation were over. Now, he could only hide or make excuses for his sudden departure.

A million thoughts occupied the mind of the 24-year-old bachelor. Katie was at the top of the list and he agonized over what it would mean to their relationship. He loved the Willamette sophomore, despite her emotional problems, but being fired from the university would make everything more complicated. He would have to move on, get another job, away from Salem — somewhere where word of his indiscretions was unknown.

Hardgrove looked up at Anne Miller, his blue eyes riveted on hers. He drew his lips inward in a pensive manner; his lashes blinked rapidly reacting to the emotion that was building behind them. He stroked the pink sheet back and forth contemplating his future.

"Anne," he said, "I thought we were friends. I never expected you to do something like this."

Anne Miller tried to hold back her own tears as she answered her colleague.

"Frank, I never thought that you would put me in this position. I thought we were friends too. I trusted you and you let me down. I thought my lecture would have given you fair warning. But when I saw the two of you still carrying on, I had no choice."

Frank heard the words of his boss and knew she was right. His heart ached, for he knew what his dismissal would mean both for himself and for Katie.

How is Katie going to react when I tell her I've got to leave town? he asked himself.

Chapter 19 – Farewell

The note was short and to the point.

Please have Katie Cole report to the Guidance Department office at 1 p.m.

It was signed Franklin Hardgrove, Guidance Counselor.

Felicia Sanchez thanked the courier and read the short note a second time. The Spanish instructor walked to the far-left side of the classroom and approached Katie, who was busily translating a chapter from *Viajes Fantásticos*, a novel by Elías Miguel Muñoz. The instructor placed the folded note on Katie's desk and whispered in her student's ear.

"The guidance counselor wants to see you; is everything okay?"

Katie put her pen down and picked up the square note, noting the Willamette school logo on the front. She opened it and read the short message. She could feel her heart skip.

What now? she thought to herself.

"I...I don't know," she answered Sanchez who was still looking over her shoulder.

"I...don't know," she repeated still reading the note.

"You can finish that later. Class is almost over. Go find out what they want." Sanchez nodded her head sharply to the right, signaling Katie to be on her way.

The collegian placed her book and pen in her knapsack and slung it over her shoulder before standing in her seat.

"Thank you," Katie said apologetically, as she walked out of the classroom.

She walked down the dimly lit hallway thinking about her disastrous weekend with Frank. She spent all day Sunday crying and was emotionally exhausted. She hadn't heard from him since Saturday night and surmised the note had something to do with it.

What else could be said? she wondered. She was not in the mood for further explanations, or for that matter begging for his love.

I know what he thinks of me...probably thinks I'm crazy and doesn't want to get involved. I can feel it – this is the kiss-off.

She stood outside Hardgrove's office and hesitated before entering. She heard the clacking of a keyboard and recognized the familiar sound. He was obviously working on his computer. The window was opaque but she could see his silhouette.

Funny, she thought, *how people behind closed doors think they can't be seen.*

Katie wrapped twice before opening the office door. She stood at the entrance waiting to be recognized. Frank looked up from the keyboard, leaving his amended resume on the computer screen. He acted surprised to see Katie.

"Hi, you're early," he said looking up at his clock.

"Yes, my teacher let me out. She thought it might be something important."

"Yes, it is – very important. Please sit down."

Frank swiveled his creaky chair to the front of his desk and showed Katie the white envelope with the pink slip inside.

"You know what this is?" he asked.

Katie shook her head.

"It's a notice of termination – I've been fired!"

"Fired...for what?"

"For being stupid, that's what," Frank fired back angrily.

"I thought Anne Miller was cool with us. I never expected her to turn on me."

"But I thought...Katie started to speak."

Frank interrupted.

"She told me I violated the confidentiality and ethical rules of the department and that I embarrassed the university. I have to clear my desk by Friday afternoon."

Katie's eyes filled with tears. She struggled to say something.

"What happens now? What about us?"

"I have an opportunity back East in Virginia...my old high school. My friend, George Secouris, is negotiating for me."

Katie heard the reply, but was puzzled. He didn't answer her question. The tears mounted and finally spilled from her eyelids.

"What about us?" she asked again, sobbing.

Frank looked straight at Katie's swollen eyes and his anger turned to compassion.

"I love you, Katie," he said sincerely.

"You have to understand. I need to think about supporting myself. No one will hire me out here. With my reputation, I'll be lucky if they hire me back in Virginia. Once I get myself situated, I promise I will call for you."

Katie wiped her tears with her sleeve. Frank wasn't giving her any options.

"Let me come with you. I have some money from my father..."

Frank interrupted.

"No, I've already done enough damage to you. I want you to finish school. You'll see, everything will work out."

Frank stood up and walked to the front of his desk. He kneeled next to Katie and kissed her hand. Tears came to the counselor's blue eyes and he wept on her lap. Katie stroked the top of her lover's head and cried with him. In her heart, she felt the relationship ending.

Chapter 20 – Time Goes By

Frank left Salem on Saturday, the day after his official termination date. He flew to Arlington, Virginia where he found a one-bedroom apartment in Fairfax, a bustling D.C. suburb about 13 miles from his intended position at Arlington High School. Fortunately, Dudley didn't remember his old antics or hear of his recent improprieties. He hired the young educator to fill the school's vacancy in the guidance department.

Frank called Katie regularly, filling her in on his doings and taking an interest in hers. However, his promises to bring her East failed to materialize. As the weeks passed, Frank's calls tapered off. Katie thought she was prepared for the breakup – she expected it, but she was heartbroken nonetheless.

Christmas came and there was no call from Frank. Two days of continuous snowfall provided an idyllic white Christmas Eve for the residents of Salem, except for Katie Cole, who spent the night crying herself to sleep. Depressed and sleep-deprived, she blamed her early morning nausea on her emotions.

Christmas was yet another reminder of her father's passing and the absence of that incestuous attention she mistakenly understood as love. Katie awoke looking for that warm body that inappropriately occupied the other side of her bed for so many years. The therapy she received at school had only brushed the surface of the emotional damage done. Her brief and unsuccessful relationship with Frank only served to emphasize the value of the permanency attached to the improper kinship with her father. Katie suffered, trying to separate herself from the contradictory feelings that confuse those in an abusive relationship.

**

The morning nausea continued to plague Katie and after missing several days of school, she began to worry that her illness was more than emotional. She didn't have a regular physician so she did what she always did when she was ill – she went to the Mill Valley Patient Care, an intermediate care facility just a half mile from the saw mill.

Katie waited patiently in the small curtained cubicle that served as an examining room. The doctor was Indian, not Native American, but from the country of India. She wore a colorful sarong and a red bindi dot on her forehead. Her hair was jet black, braided and pinned back against her head. Around her neck, she balanced a doubled up stethoscope. A nametag identified her as Rupa Majhi, M.D.

Dr. Majhi entered the cubicle with a big grin. A glint of gold shone from some dental work obviously performed by an Indian dentist.

"Well, I've got good news for you," she said in broken English.

"Good news?" Katie couldn't imagine how feeling nauseous could be good news.

"Yes, you are pregnant," the doctor said ignoring her patient's ignorance.

"Pregnant...but, how?" Katie asked in amazement.

The doctor laughed. She had heard the question many times before.

"Well let me see," she answered, still smiling. "The only way that I know how is when..."

Katie stopped her. Suddenly, she was embarrassed.

"Okay, I know about the birds and the bees," she said shyly.

"The birds and what?" the doctor replied, showing her unfamiliarity with American colloquialisms.

Now it was Katie's turn to laugh. She did and then followed it up with tears.

"When?" she inquired, wiping her eyes.

The doctor looked at her chart and began counting on her fingers.

"I'm not an obstetrician but it looks like the middle of June. You should see your gynecologist for an exact date."

Katie peered at the Indian doctor through her tears. The bright colors of the sarong danced and blended like beads in a kaleidoscope. The scene in front of her was blurred but her memories were clear. She remembered the night it happened; a wonderful loving moment that suddenly erupted into something horrific.

It's Frank's baby, she thought to herself. *I can't believe it. I'm going to be a mother and he's going to be a father. But should I tell him?*

Chapter 21 – A Professional Referral

It was Tuesday, January 4, 1994 and school was back in session. The day was overcast; a gray sky full of snow clouds hung over the university. It was cold, very cold, about 20 degrees, with a cutting wind blowing out of the northeast. Dr. Anne Miller from the Guidance Department summoned Katie to her office.

She walked through the star grove of bare sequoias towards the school entrance. Her shoulders were hunched and the collar of her black wool coat was up, protecting her neck from the harsh cold. Her mouth and nose were buried in a red crocheted scarf that she received as a Christmas gift from her friend Laura.

She pulled on the brass handle of the university door and held it open against the stiff wind that tried equally hard to shut it. The door slammed shut as Katie entered the warmth of the hallway. She shivered as she made her way to the counselor's office. It was a rather long walk and, by the time she entered the psychologist's office, her body began to thaw.

"Hi Katie," Dr. Miller greeted her client. "I'm so sorry. How long has it been – maybe two months since I last saw you?"

"Yeah, I guess," she responded, placing her knapsack on the floor and removing her coat.

"I'm sorry for the delay, but with my international conferences and the holidays, my schedule was completely thrown out of kilter."

Katie sat down wondering how to respond to this woman who didn't seem to give a damn about her; who thwarted her relationship and left her pregnant without a husband to help rear her child. The thoughts came rapidly and the more she looked at the educator, the angrier she became.

"Before we get started Katie, I want to explain a few things."

You, you...you've got more than a little explaining, Katie thought to herself. *You took my Frank away from me.*

Dr. Miller saw the anger in Katie's face. She was trained to observe and understand body language: the tight jaw, the clenched fist, the dilated pupils, and the reddish face – all signs she understood.

"I know you must think awful of me for getting Mr. Hardgrove fired. I know that you and he...well that you were having a relationship."

"You don't know anything," Katie burst out crying. "I'm pregnant and now Frank is in Virginia, 3,000 miles away. He hasn't called me in weeks and my baby won't have a father."

Katie pounded the table and tears flooded her face. Dr. Miller listened intently to her client's ranting. It was healthy for Katie to let it out – to release all those pent up feelings. She couldn't blame the innocent co-ed for her anger. It was a natural reaction to lash out at the messenger. Yes, she delivered the pink slip to Hardgrove's desk, but it was he who brought it on himself.

Miller waited while Katie vented. She knew it was useless to interrupt. When the sobbing subsided and Katie could hear and understand her words, Miller continued.

"Katie, I understand your anger and your disappointment. I know this is a very difficult time for you. Being pregnant is hard enough for a woman with a committed partner...does he know?"

Katie shook her head. She wiped her eyes with a tissue she garnered from the psychologist's desk.

"What am I going to do," she asked in frustration.

"Maybe you should tell him," Miller suggested.

"I don't want him for that...he doesn't love me...he thinks I'm crazy."

"Crazy?" Miller looked confused. "What makes you say that?"

Katie had said too much. She didn't want to explain. It was embarrassing. How could she tell her what was eating her up inside? The nightmares, the visions, the perverted sex – it was all part of the craziness, the part she couldn't talk about.

Dr. Miller listened to the words and watched Katie's actions, recalling their previous sessions together. Suddenly, the meaning revealed itself and she understood. This was a tough one – certainly more than could be expected of a guidance counselor. Katie needed professional help.

Miller opened her desk drawer and pulled a business card from a stack of others. The card had the name Stephanie Solz, M.D. imprinted in the center.

"Katie, this is a very good friend of mine," Miller held the card in front of her client. "I want you to see her as soon as possible. I know you don't have money, but don't be concerned about that; she will see you pro-bono on my recommendation."

Pro-bono, what does that mean? Katie asked herself. She looked at the card. The words *Clinical Psychiatry* stood out boldly.

Sure, now she believes it too. Pretty soon everyone will think I'm crazy.

Chapter 22 – A New Beginning

Laura Sunshine knocked heavily on the white door of the small cottage on Winona Drive. Desperate and cold, she waited anxiously for Katie to come to her rescue. The 5-foot dark-haired half-breed had her head and shoulders covered by a red and black woven blanket, which she held tightly around her small frame. She shivered in the doorway feeling the bite of the wind and the cold of the newly driven snow against her cheeks. Katie opened the door to find her friend in tears.

"Laura, what is it? What's wrong?" she asked.

"We had a fight," she said, barely able to move her mouth.

Katie closed the thinly insulated door and ushered Laura into her living room. A thick log burned brightly in a small stone hearth sending waves of heat into the small cottage. Katie took the snow-covered blanket from Laura and placed it on a clothes rack that sat near the flaming fireplace.

The two friends took seats at opposite ends of the single upholstered sofa.

"Can I make you some tea?" Katie asked, trying to comfort Laura.

"Thank you, I could use something to warm up. It's freezing outside," Laura said, still shivering.

Katie walked to the small kitchen and filled a copper kettle with water. She lit the small gas stove and placed the teapot on the burner.

"So, what happened?" Katie said, walking back into the living room.

"Katie, I can't stand it anymore. He's never home and I'm sure he's running around. When I'm home or off from work, I get these weird phone calls; hang-ups from the same number. I tried using star-69 to trace the calls and some bimbo answers the phone. When I ask her name, she hangs up on me. I confronted him last night and we had a huge fight. I spent most of the night driving around the city. I left with five dollars in my wallet. I can't even fill my gas tank."

Laura began to cry as the teapot whistled in the other room. Katie took note of the high pitched sound and heeded its call. She steeped an herbal teabag in a ceramic mug filled with boiling water. After adding a teaspoon of honey, she brought the steaming drink into the living room and handed it to Laura. Katie sat back on the sofa and listened to her friend's lament before giving her opinion.

"I'm really sorry Laura, I don't know Sam all that well, but he seems like a nice guy. I guess men are never satisfied with what they have."

Katie was reminded of her own circumstances and she pondered whether to bring it up.

"I don't know what I'm going to do Katie," Laura said, sipping her tea. "I'm tired of fighting with him – he's driving me crazy."

Laura's words reminded Katie once again of her situation with Frank. She longed to share her feelings with her cherished friend, but decided to wait.

"Laura, why don't you stay with me for a few days, until you get yourself settled?" Katie suggested.

Katie moved closer and clasped the hand of her good friend. She knew how it felt to be alone and scared.

"You are so good – I don't deserve you," Laura said, wiping her tears. "Where would I stay? I mean your house is so small. You don't have room for me."

"I can set up a cot in my bedroom. It's only a temporary arrangement until you can find your own place. Look, it will be good for me too. I could use the company. You can drive me to school and save me from waiting at the bus stop. It's so cold out there."

Laura finished the last drop of her tea and placed the empty mug in her lap. She thought about the generous offer and considered the alternatives.

Laura thought it out quickly. *If I go back to Sam, it will only be more of the same. Maybe a few days of being without me will make him see the light.*

"Okay," she said, smiling through her tears. "You have a deal, but only till I find myself a place."

Chapter 23 – Bible Class

The Mill Creek Mission Church held Bible study every Tuesday and Thursday evenings between 6 and 8 p.m. Because loggers comprised most of the congregation, and because as a rule, they spent their nights recovering from the toil of the day, the classes were sparsely attended. Katie was not a regular attendee, but on occasion, when she felt the need for some spiritual inspiration, she walked down to the small mission and sat in on a class.

Katie, feeling especially dispirited after an all day bout with morning sickness, decided she needed some fresh air. She grabbed her Bible and set out towards the church. A one-inch layer of frozen snow covered the ground. Each step produced a crunching sound that seemed particularly loud on the quiet street.

The Methodist chapel was about a mile or so from Katie's home. She walked briskly breathing in the chilled winter air. She hadn't eaten the entire day and, although she felt some weakness, she had no hunger. The walking exercise was good for her soul and also helped her queasiness.

It took Katie 20 minutes to reach her destination. She peered into the mission's classroom before entering. She immediately recognized Sarah Singleton, the religious affairs director, leading the session. There appeared to be four women and one man sitting in the wooden desk chairs.

Katie slowly closed the classroom door trying not to disturb the discussion. She walked to the second row of desks and took a seat behind the only man in the room. She opened her bible and leaned forward over the male student's shoulder in front of her. As she strained to see the page number, the faint scent of his cologne floated past her nostrils. Unlike Frank's sweet citrus essence, that sent her into ecstasy, this scent was harsh and alcoholic and actually repelled her.

Sarah, noticing Katie, welcomed her to the class.

"Hi Katie, welcome to our bible study. We're discussing the Gospel of Luke. We are at chapter 23, verse 46. Jesus is on the cross and is about to expire. The verse reads as follows: 'And when Jesus had cried with a loud voice, he said, Father, into thy hands I commend my spirit: and having said thus, he gave up the ghost.' I would like an interpretation as to these words."

The man sitting in front of Katie raised his hand. Sarah nodded her head, recognizing the student.

"I think that Jesus knew he was dying and he was offering his soul up to God."

Katie listened to the words of the familiar voice but wasn't sure of his identity. She leaned to the side of her desk taking in the profile of the gentlemen. He had a full head of hair and a matching beard that was trimmed close to his face. His nose was straight and strong; his lips were thin. Suddenly, the profile turned into a full face as the man felt Katie's stare and turned towards her. Embarrassed, Katie returned to an upright position.

"Hi," the man whispered to the figure behind him.

Katie's faced turned red as she recognized the good-looking man. It was Josh McCreary, the church organist, the same talented musician she recognized at the amphitheater on her second date with Frank. The memory of the evening was clear. McCreary was part of the group known as *The Rivermen*. Katie remembered reading his name in the playbill and the thrill of seeing him on stage.

"Yes," Sarah Singleton, replied, noticing the exchange between her students. "The ghost refers to the spirit or the soul. *To give up the ghost*, means to give up the spirit or the soul or to give up the breath, to expire or die."

Josh turned back to the voice of the instructor and acknowledged her statement with an understanding nod.

Katie tried following the class discussion but her mind kept focusing on Frank and her baby. The religious director caught Katie daydreaming and out of respect, avoided calling on her.

Sarah Singleton was no stranger to Katie or her widowed father. She had taught school in the church for 20 years and knew Katie as a little girl. After class, the religious director approached Katie, asking if everything was okay. The mother-to-be reacted with surprise at the bible leader's intuitiveness.

"Oh, Ms. Singleton" she said, "I didn't realize it was so obvious. I have a lot of things on my mind and I haven't been feeling well today."

Sarah was very much in touch with the tragedies that had befallen the Cole family and over the years she took a special interest in the widower's daughter. During the latter years before the accident, the word has gotten around that Jack was drinking. Concern over Katie's welfare led the religious leader to ask for Jack's participation in the mission's 12-step program. When he refused, she notified Salem's Child Protective Services. At the time, Katie was 16. Because of her age, the city refused to get involved, claiming they had no jurisdiction.

Sarah watched Katie rub her stomach as she described her discomfort and wondered if her bible student had something more than anxiety and an upset stomach. The paleness in her face and the slight bulge in her midsection made the seasoned teacher wonder if indeed, Katie wasn't pregnant.

The 19-year-old excused herself and walked to the classroom's exit door. She stepped outside into the cold winter air and took a deep breath before charting her way home.

Chapter 24 – A Walk Home

Katie clutched her bible with a gloved hand and began the one-mile trek home. She was only a half-block from the church when she heard the sound of footsteps closing in behind her. It was Josh McCreary and he was running to catch up.

"Katie, wait up," he hollered.

The young musician was panting and his warm breath condensed in the cold, producing a cloud of vapor that hung in the air like a fog.

"How are you," he asked, still breathing heavily.

"Fine, I didn't know you took bible class."

"That makes two of us," Josh answered. "Mind if I walk you home?"

"Isn't it out of your way," Katie replied.

"I'm heading in the same direction; it's not a big deal. So, are you still at Willamette?"

"Yeah, I am but I don't know for how long," Katie replied, anxious to share her secret with someone.

"Why is that? Are you leaving town?" McCreary asked.

"No, I still have two years until I graduate, but..." Katie hesitated.

Should I tell him? she thought to herself. *He hardly knows me – but I think I can be open with him.*

"I'm going to have a baby," she blurted the declaration out, smiling broadly.

Josh stopped in his tracks and instinctively looked down at Katie's stomach, expecting to see a sign of the human life growing behind the wool coat.

"I'm not showing much," Katie laughed. "I'm only in my third month. You're the first one I've told."

"Really, what about the lucky father?" Josh asked, stroking his beard.

"His name is...George," Katie lied, protecting his identity. "He doesn't know yet."

"Oh?" Josh answered, inquisitively. "But why? How come you haven't told him?"

"I'm not sure if I'm going to see him again. He left town for a new job. If he returns to Salem or calls for me, then I will tell him."

Josh walked in silence with Katie, contemplating the disclosure while feeling her vulnerability.

"So, how are you going to support yourself? Do you have a job?" Josh asked.

"No…I guess I'm going to have to get one. If I quit Willamette, I will lose my scholarship and the spending money they pay me. It's called a stipend.

"Our house is paid for and I don't spend much. I've been living off the money my father left me, but there's not much left."

"You know this is really ironic," Josh broke in. "The reason, I asked to walk you home was…well, I wanted to talk to you about our band."

"Your band?" Katie turned to her walking partner, doubtful of his statement. "You must be kidding. What would I do in a band? I don't play an instrument."

"No, no," Josh laughed out loud. "This is not about instruments. Actually when I saw you in class, it refreshed my memory of when we sang together in the church choir. I think we were about 11 or 12 years old. You probably don't even remember. I have to tell you that I had a secret crush on you."

Katie laughed, waiting to hear the rest of the line.

"It's true, I really liked you; but that was a long time ago. You know I'm married now?"

"No, I didn't know that," Katie replied, thinking *how would I know that?*

"Yes, we have a one-year-old little boy named Sean. He was named after my grandfather."

"Ah, that's wonderful Josh, I'm sure you're very happy...so then, what about your band? Why did you want to talk to me?"

"Oh yes, we are looking for someone to be our M.C.; to introduce us and participate in some of our numbers. When I saw you in class, I thought you would be perfect for us. You're pretty and you have a nice voice. Peggy Rice, our former M.C., got married and moved out of state. So, we don't have anyone at this time. It's unprofessional introducing ourselves, if you know what I mean."

"Josh, I'm starting to show, Katie said, looking down. In a few months, I'll be big as a house. How could I be your M.C. in that condition?"

"I don't see that as a problem. In fact, I think it would be very nice to have you up on the stage dressed in fancy maternity clothes. Times are very different; people don't regard pregnancy as shameful any more. I know year's ago, women used to hide their condition, but not today."

"I'll have to think on that, Josh," Katie said, envisioning herself on the stage.

The couple continued walking and talking. Katie enjoyed Josh's company and felt very much at ease discussing things. In a way, she was glad that Josh was married and had a baby. She saw this as an opportunity for a new male friendship – one that she wouldn't fear.

Josh walked Katie to her doorstep and waited while she searched for her key. As she turned to say goodnight, Josh was in her face. Startled, she tried to turn away, but Josh pulled her back into his arms. He kissed her passionately on the lips before Katie had a chance to realize the advance. Katie struggled against the prickly beard that scratched her cold chapped face with a vengeance. Josh pressed his body harder into hers, trying to overcome her resistance. Suddenly, old memories of abuse filled her mind and Katie struggled strenuously against the familiar force she had known before. She struck out with her fists and instinctively kneed Josh in the groin.

The bible student went down onto the frozen ground, clutching his privates and writhing in pain. Just as he did, the door to the small cottage opened. Laura stood in the doorway. Seeing the man on the ground and sensing the gravity of the situation, she pulled Katie inside, slamming the wooden door in the face of her attacker.

Chapter 25 – A Necessary Move

Katie slept uneasy, her dreams filled with scary images of men ripping at her clothes. She struggled through the night, tossing and turning, fighting off the dark figures with no faces. When daylight finally made its way into her bedroom, she awoke feeling restless and weary. Immediately, she recalled her previous night's encounter with Josh McCreary. The incident replayed itself; she could feel the sharp bristles of his beard tearing against her cold cheeks, his lips seeking a response, his body forcing its way against her swollen stomach. The ruminations were painful. She buried her head in her pillow trying to block out the memory. It was then that she realized she needed help.

**

Katie searched her purse for the small business card that Dr. Anne Miller gave her. It was at the bottom, wedged between her compact and a tube of lipstick. She read the information and recalled the name of the psychiatric nurse. According to Dr. Miller, Stephanie Solz was a personal friend of the school counselor-head. She remembered her saying, 'don't worry about her fees.' *That was good,* she thought. *I can't afford to pay any fees.*

Katie dialed the 10-digit number and waited for an answer.

"Salem Hospital, may I help you?" the operator announced.

"Yes, I would like to speak with Dr. Solz' office," Katie replied, unaware that Stephanie Solz was not an M.D.

The operator put Katie on hold while she connected the call.

"Dr. Arnat's office," the receptionist answered.

"Oh, I must have the wrong number," Katie replied. "I was looking for Dr. Solz."

The receptionist was prepared.

"You have the correct number. Nurse Solz is a psychiatric nurse practitioner. She works with Dr. Arnat. Would you like to make an appointment with her?"

"Oh, yes – when can I get to see her. I am not feeling very well."

"May I ask who referred you?" the receptionist asked.

"Yes, Dr. Miller, Dr. Anne Miller from Willamette University."

The receptionist placed Katie on hold while she checked her appointment book.

"Nurse Solz can see you at 1 p.m. tomorrow. How does that sound?"

Katie thought for a moment and then replied.

"That's good. I don't have any insurance," she warned.

The receptionist listened to the trepidation in Katie's voice, but was prepared.

"You needn't be concerned about that. Students from Willamette are treated gratis."

"I guess that means free?" Katie questioned the secretary.

"That's correct," the receptionist answered sweetly. "We're affiliated with Willamette."

Katie hung up the phone and stared out her bedroom window wondering if she would ever feel normal.

**

Stephanie Solz counseled her patients at the Salem Hospital, where she shared an office with Dr. Robert Arnat, a renowned Nobel Prize-winning psychiatrist.

Katie, bundled in a wool coat, scarf, hat and gloves, left her Spanish class a few minutes early to meet her 1 p.m. appointment. The hospital was a short walk from the university, but the bitter cold made even the briefest trek an ordeal. With a temperature of 22 degrees and winds at 5 miles per hour, it felt like only 15 degrees to the stocking-capped student.

The hospital entrance looked like any other with a revolving front door that helped shield the inside from the bitter cold blasts of air. Several uniformed security guards stood beyond the door, providing badges to all visitors. An information clerk sat behind a polished marble wall giving out directions.

Katie showed the clerk the calling card of Nurse Solz and was pointed to the bank of elevators just south of the information desk. She rode the modern elevator to the third floor accompanied by a little old lady that resembled one of the aunts from *Arsenic and Old Lace*. The Willamette student stepped out of the elevator leaving the macabre-looking passenger huddled in the corner of the lift. *I wonder if her next victim is located on the fifth floor*, she thought, containing her laugh.

Dr. Arnat's office was bright and cheery, with mustard colored walls and light green accents. One could immediately see a decorator's touch at work in the multi-room suite. Katie approached the glass enclosed reception area and introduced herself to the young secretary, speaking through the glass window that seemed more appropriate in a liquor store than a doctor's office.

Suddenly, the glass panel moved to the side and the secretary handed the new patient a clipboard full of papers. She instructed Katie to fill out the forms and return them, along with the pharmaceutical pen that was securely fastened to the board with a chain of metal beads.

Katie looked at her watch. It was 1:05 p.m. She had just started filling out the multitude of forms and questionnaires, when Nurse Solz entered the waiting area.

"Katie Cole?" she queried the patients waiting their turn.

"Here," Katie raised her hand as she did in school.

The psychiatric nurse approached the source of the acknowledgement and greeted her new patient.

"Hi Katie, I'm Stephanie Solz. I'm so glad to meet you. Won't you come in to my office?"

Katie hesitated unsure of what to do with her clipboard of forms.

"You can fill that out later," Nurse Solz said smiling. "Here let me take that from you. My office is just down this corridor."

Katie immediately took a liking to the maternal looking counselor. She appeared to be in her 50's but her gray hair pulled back in a bun, certainly made her seem older. She was dressed simply in a patterned frock. With the exception of a barely visible lipstick line, she wore no facial makeup. A small butterfly pin attached to her dress was the only noticeable adornment.

The long corridor had many offices, some with sophisticated equipment that looked too high-tech for a psychiatric office. The sight of the machines made Katie a little apprehensive.

I wonder if they fry people's brains with those things, she thought, remembering something she once read.

Nurse Solz' office was at the end of the corridor. It, like the front office, was bright and cheery painted with pastel colors. Some abstract paintings resembling Rorschach inkblots hung on the walls. Katie studied the drawings and wondered if the nurse was going to use them on her.

Nurse Solz flicked a switch on a small machine in the corner of her office and a fan-like whirring sound emanated from the device.

"Oh, don't let that bother you," Solz said, seeing Katie's concern. "Just some white background noise to prevent people from listening in."

Katie took a seat in a tufted brown armchair that hugged the corner of the office. It was plush and cushy and when she sat, she wondered how she would ever get out. Nurse Solz sat opposite her patient in a straight back chair that was similarly upholstered but not nearly as cushy. The psychiatric nurse spoke first.

"Well Katie, I'm so glad to meet you. I see where my friend Anne Miller has referred you. She is a terrific lady – very gifted and very competent. Do you know why she referred you to me?"

Katie shrugged her shoulders, but knew better. She waited a few seconds and when Nurse Solz didn't answer, she followed up with a better reply.

"I guess because my problems were too much for her to handle."

"I wouldn't say they were too much. I'd rather say that I was better trained to handle them." Solz replied.

"Why don't we start from the beginning. Tell me about your childhood."

Katie sighed. She knew it would come to this. *How many times do I have to repeat the same story*, she thought to herself. *I guess I'll have to tell it all this time.*

Chapter 26 – The East Coast

Franklin Hardgrove sat at his new desk thinking about Katie and their last conversation. He hadn't talked with her in weeks. When he last called, she was belligerent and accusatory. She didn't seem herself; she reproached him, saying he was cowardly and full of himself. She blamed him for not being understanding and accused him of running away from his responsibilities. Frank didn't like or understand the tone of the conversation. This was so unlike Katie. He never knew her to be belligerent or accusatory. When Katie hung up on him, he was stunned and his pride hurt. Frank thought the matter out and decided that he was entitled to an apology. He would not call Katie until he received one.

**

His first month at Arlington High School was trying for the college-trained counselor. Working with high school students was totally different and required a new level of patience and understanding. The students at Arlington were especially rebellious and reluctant to discuss their personal affairs. Many of his sessions were more like detention, with students sitting in silence, staring him down. The few that were willing to speak did so disrespectfully, using four-letter words as casually as drunken sailors on a weekend pass. The experience was demeaning to the educated UVA graduate and after only a month, he was ready to move on.

**

It was Friday evening and Hardgrove was in his apartment feeling restless. Four weeks had passed since he spoke with Katie. He thought often of the angelic face that he'd come to love in the course of just a few months at Willamette. He recalled their times together and loneliness set in. He wished he could be there with her, holding her close, kissing her warm lips and inhaling the fragrant smell of jasmine that set his body on fire.

Frank thought about Katie's accusations and his self-promise to wait for an apology. *This is ridiculous*, he thought to himself. *Obviously, I am not going to receive an apology. I am cutting off my nose to spite my face*, he thought again.

He picked up the telephone and stared at the dial pad. He had to think a minute trying to remember the once familiar number that now appeared somewhat dim in his memory. He tapped out the number, then stopped and pressed the flash button, wondering if he was doing right. The counselor took a deep breath and dialed the full number. *What the hell,* he thought, *nothing ventured, nothing gained.*

Frank tapped his foot nervously as the ringing began.

"Hello," Laura answered the phone.

"Hi, Katie, is that you?"

"This is Laura. Did you want Katie?"

"Oh, hi Laura. I've heard a lot about you. This is Frank Hardgrove. Is she there?"

"Hold on." Laura put her hand over the phone and whispered Frank's name.

Katie placed the *Parents Magazine* on the sofa and looked toward the kitchen where Laura stood holding the receiver.

"It's him – Frank," she whispered again, this time a little louder.

Katie shook her head. "Tell him I don't want to talk to him," she said, half-heartedly.

Laura continued to hold her hand to the phone. She beckoned Katie using the phone as a pointer.

"Don't be silly, talk to him," she said louder.

Frank heard the muffled remark on the other end and was puzzled. *Why doesn't she want to talk to me? Why is she so angry?* he thought to himself.

Katie, prodded by her friend's insistence, rose from the sofa and walked to the kitchen. She grimaced slightly as she took the phone to her ear.

"Yes," she said coldly.

"Katie, it's me," Frank said meekly. "Can we talk?"

"What is there to talk about Frank?" Katie answered matter-of-factly "I'm here and you're there and I don't see where there's anything to talk about."

"I miss you. I want to see you."

"You miss me so much that you haven't called me in four weeks." Katie answered sarcastically.

"I'm sorry, I didn't think you..."

"What Frank, you didn't think what?" Katie said, holding back the tears.

Frank heard her voice breaking and felt his eyes well up. Hearing her sweet voice made him long for her even more. He spoke with compassion.

"Sweetheart, I really miss you. I'm miserable here without you. I hate my job...I want to be with you."

"I wanted to be with you too Frank, but you left me here alone. I'm not sure that you really meant all the things you said, Frank. Besides, you wouldn't want me now anyhow – not in my condition."

"Your condition...?" Frank asked. "What are you talking about?"

Katie didn't mean to say it. It just slipped out. She bit her tongue and winced.

"Nothing, I didn't mean to say that."

Frank heard the trepidation and knew something was wrong. Suddenly, he started to put the pieces together. *Whatever was troubling her was why she turned on me. All the accusations, all the emotion; that's why she hung up on me*, Frank reasoned.

"Katie, you've got to tell me – whatever it is, we'll work it out together. Please talk to me," he begged.

"Okay, you want to know, I'll tell you…then we'll see how anxious you are to be with me."

Frank listened for the bombshell wondering how bad it was going to be.

Was she sick – did she have cancer; was she going to die?

Katie could almost feel the anticipation in Frank's pause. She swallowed hard trying to get the words out. Finally she said it.

"I'm pregnant Frank…with your baby."

Frank held the phone in his hand unable to speak. The shock of the news left him speechless. *She's pregnant*, he thought. *Oh, my God, but how? She said it was my baby.* The questions came so quickly, that Frank was tongue-tied. Silence filled the room as the impact of the admission hit home.

Katie picked up on the pause, the silence, and felt the shock on the other end. She slammed the phone down and ran crying to her room.

"I knew it," she said sobbing. "He isn't interested in me. Why should he be – he thinks I've made it up... doesn't believe he's the father. God, I hate him."

Katie clutched her pillow as the tears poured from her eyes. She cried uncontrollably, sobbing, shuttering, and unable to catch her breath. Laura came into the small bedroom and sat on the edge of the bed. Katie was curled up in a fetal position. Laura stroked the back of her head and whispered Indian incantations to sooth her friend's despair.

The soft chanting found its way to Katie's ears. Like the soothing sounds of a lullaby, the Indian song calmed Katie. Her sobbing subsided. Laura stretched out next to Katie and continued her mantra-like chant. Within minutes, both roommates were asleep.

It was an emotional Friday evening. The air was charged with fears and doubts. With no way to resolve them, it was better to give way to sleep, and give uncertainty a rest. And so they did, until the early hours of the morning when new revelations came to pass.

Chapter 27 – Decisions

Frank stood dumbfounded holding the phone receiver in his hand, listening to the drone of a dial tone 3,000 miles away.

My God, he thought, *I'm going to be a father*.

He placed the receiver on the cradle and leaned back on the upholstered wing chair that sat alone in the barren living room. His mind raced with a thousand thoughts, weaving a pattern of both joy and anxiety. He closed his eyes, listening to the thoughts that inundated his mind.

In between the ruminations, Frank recalled how it happened.

It was that night at the inn at Detroit Lake. How could I forget it? I remember lying there in her arms, kissing her hot lips, breathing in the sweet smell of jasmine, enjoying the pleasure of her warm body against mine. It felt so good being a part of her – giving myself to her and she to me. Oh, God, I remember it all, everything, including the climactic pinnacle. Yes, that was the best and the worst of it. I was 10,000 miles away on a deserted island, just Katie and me locked in an eternal embrace. Then the Tsunami came in the form of fists beating on me like distant drums. I was drained and the screams that accompanied the pounding were no more than loud voices bent on subverting my pleasure and satisfaction. I tried to subdue the interruption, consenting to the physical and emotional ecstasy that drew me deeper into the Garden of Eden, but it was a futile attempt.

The drums were too strong and the voices too loud. I was suddenly roused from the strong undercurrents of the giant wave carrying me out to sea. I lay there breathless, trying to gain a sense of the reality that shattered my fantasy. My brain, blurred and sedated suddenly began to process the messages being sent in rapid succession.

It was Katie, beating on me, shouting for me to get off of her. Yes, I remember it all. That's how it happened.

Frank opened his eyes and everything was crystal clear. He was going to be a father; he remembered how and when it occurred. Now, he would have to come to terms with it.

Chapter 28 – Misunderstandings

It was a little past 8 a.m. when the phone rang in the small cottage. Laura opened her eyes surprised to see someone in bed with her. By the second ring, she remembered how she got there and sat up. The phone continued ringing. Katie stirred, groaned and placed her pillow over her head. It was obvious, Katie wasn't a bit interested in the phone call. Laura put her feet on the cold floor and reached for the phone.

"Hello," Laura spoke sleepily.

"Hi…this is Frank, is that you Laura?"

"Yes, Frank, it's awfully early for you to call," Laura admonished the long distance caller.

"Katie is still sleeping and I don't think she wants to talk to you anymore. You really upset her last night."

"Oh my God, I am so sorry. She hung up the phone before I had a chance to say anything. I was so stunned by the news, I didn't know what to say. I guess she misunderstood my silence. I need to talk with her. Can you please tell her I'm on the phone?"

"Frank, I know she won't talk with you and I think you are wasting your time. You have already caused enough damage – why don't you just leave her alone? It's hard enough without you rocking the boat."

Frank heard the anger in Laura's voice. It was all a big mistake. She wasn't giving him a chance to talk and say what he had called about. Frustrated by the phone highjack, Frank lost it. He yelled into his mouthpiece.

"Listen to me Laura, and don't hang up the phone. I want to say something so please allow me to express myself."

"Go on," Laura stood at the foot of the bed tapping her foot.

Frank took a deep breath before replying. He thought about how much he missed Katie and how much she meant to him. His tone changed immediately.

"Laura, you tell Katie that I love her and that I am coming back to Salem. You tell her that when I come back, I want to marry her. Are you listening?"

Laura grinned and couldn't believe what she was hearing. She looked over at Katie buried under her pillow and wished she were at her side overhearing the conversation.

"I hear you Frank; go on."

"Laura, I can't wait to be with Katie. I can't believe that I'm going to be a father. When she wakes up, please tell her that I am winding up my affairs and by the weekend, I'll be in Salem. Now promise me you'll tell her all that."

"Oh Frank, she will be so happy. Maybe I should wake her."

"No, don't – she needs her rest. I will call her again tonight. It's almost noon here. As soon as I hang up, I'm going over to the rental office and settle up with them. Then I'm going to buy an airline ticket for next Saturday. On Monday, I'm going to give my notice at school. You tell her that…you make sure, okay?"

Laura heard the click of the phone before she could answer. She held the receiver in her hand replaying the conversation in her head. *I need to get all this right*, she thought to herself. *Now what exactly did he say?*

Chapter 29 – A New Day

Laura hung up the phone and turned towards Katie. She hoped to see some signs of life so she could share the wonderful news, but Katie had not budged.

Laura checked her wristwatch. It was 8:40 a.m. and the dark-haired beautician was due in to work by 9 O'clock. She looked down at her faded jeans and crumpled shirt and realized she had slept in them.

"Shit," she cursed under her breath, "I don't have time to dress."

She slipped on her beaded moccasins and made her way to the bathroom. She was in and out in less than five minutes. By 9:10 a.m., she was out the door and on her way. *I'll try to call Katie from work*, she thought, as she sped up Winona Drive.

It was 10:15a.m. when the Cole telephone rang again. Katie heard the muffled sound of the phone. At the third ring, she sat upright in her bed. She looked around and noticed Laura's empty cot. She yawned and stretched before reaching for the phone.

"Hello," she said softly, in the middle of the fourth ring.

"Katie, this is Josh McCreary calling. Please don't hang up on me."

"Josh?" Katie asked, puzzled by the phone call.

"Yes," listen Katie, I wanted to apologize for the other night. I don't know what came over me. I should have never…well you know what I mean. I'm a married man with a baby."

Katie listened to the expression of regret with reservation. *Maybe I should hang up on him. Does he really deserve my attention?* she thought, recalling the incident. *What is it with men – are they all just animals?*

"Josh, I don't know…" Katie hesitated. "I never expected that kind of thing from you."

"Katie, I know and believe me, you expressed your self very well. I'm still sore from your knee."

Katie covered her mouthpiece and giggled. *He deserved it*, she thought.

"Okay Josh, I forgive you; is there anything else?"

"As a matter of fact there is. We are still looking for someone for the band. I was hoping that maybe you might still be interested."

Katie recalled Josh's proposal and initially fretted over the idea. She couldn't see herself up on a stage while pregnant, but Josh had assured her that her condition wasn't a problem. With the baby coming, she certainly could use the money. The proposition was very interesting but it was too early in the morning for an answer. Katie hedged in replying.

"Josh, I'd like to think about it – how soon do you need an answer?"

"There's no deadline, but I know that the other guys are interviewing people. I would like you to be in the running. Besides, I owe you one and would like to make it up to you."

"You don't owe me anything Josh. I'll let you know the beginning of the week."

"That's fine, and Katie, I'd appreciate if you didn't say anything about the incident between us. We live in a very small community, you know!"

Katie's ears peeked at hearing Josh's request for silence. Suddenly she questioned the musician's motives in calling. *Did he call to apologize and offer me a job or to shut me up?*

Chapter 30 – Plans and Happenings

It was almost noon on the East Coast and Frank had a lot to do if he was going to be in Salem by the weekend. He sat in his sparse apartment making a to-do list, writing one thought at a time. As he wrote his list, he smiled with each added line.

1. *Call Claude Guilbert and arrange for car*
2. *Buy airline ticket to Salem*
3. *Make hotel reservation*
4. *Rental office – give notice and request deposit*
5. *Call furniture rental company and cancel lease*
6. *Give notice at work*
7. *Close checking account*
8. *Notify Post Office of change of address*
9. *Buy wedding band*

Before his hasty exit from Salem, Frank stored his car in a garage owned by his French friend, Claude Guilbert. As he completed the first note about retrieving the vehicle, he quickly dialed the Salem teacher. A brief conversation ensued followed by arrangements for the car to be dropped off at the airport.

Frank made his airline and motel reservations next. He then decided to tackle the rental office. His lease was month to month. It was the beginning of February and his rent for the month was due. He grabbed his lease and quickly scanned the three-page agreement. According to the terms, he was required to give 30 days notice to cancel. The complex held a month's rent as security deposit. After reading the terms a second and third time, Frank realized he might have a problem. Because he was canceling on short notice, he would be responsible for the entire month's rent. Holding back February's rent would result in a forfeiture of his security deposit.

Frank spent a great deal of money getting situated in his new job. The costs of getting to the East Coast and establishing housing there almost drained his savings account. The additional costs of returning to Salem would impact his finances again. He looked in his wallet and counted the bills. For a brief moment, he wondered if he had enough to buy an airline ticket. Then he remembered his credit card.

No problem, he thought. *I still have $1,500 left on my credit line. Besides, the rental agent seems nice* *enough. Perhaps I can charm her into working something out.*

**

It was unusually cold and blustery in Fairfax. The temperature was in the high teens and remnants of the prior day's snowstorm were visible in all directions. The rooftops were covered with 3-4 inches of snow and the streets and sidewalks had patches of ice that made driving and walking hazardous. Gusts of 20-25 mile-per-hour winds howled through the complex blowing snow in all directions. Frank donned his nylon winter parka and leather gloves and left his apartment, clutching his lease.

The Fairfax apartment complex consisted of some 300 clustered townhouse units. The rental office was located at the far end of the compound, just 100 feet from U.S. Route 29, Lee Highway.

Frank tried to shortcut the quarter-mile pavement walk between his unit and the rental office by trudging across the snowy grass lawns that connected the entire parcel of land. The trek to the rental office was no easy task. Besides fighting off the cold and the blinding snow, Frank had to watch his footing. Beneath the snowy crust, unknown hazards such as sinkholes, sewer drains and iron pipe traps lay in wait for the unwary traveler. Like mines on a battlefield, these obstacles present a clear challenge in good weather and a booby trap in bad.

Frank turned the corner of the last group of apartments and headed for the front office. Suddenly his left foot gave way. The inimitable sinkhole had made itself known. Frank's foot turned inward as it slammed into a steel storm drain hidden by a shallow bridge of snow. The howling wind and a sudden shrill scream obscured the sound of all three-ankle-bones shattering below the frozen landscape. Frank fell to the ground writhing in pain. His lease no longer of concern, he released his grip on the agreement. The wind carried the document high into the air, across Lee Highway and into the path of the oncoming traffic. The document separated and its three pages were torn to shreds as car after car hammered the legal instrument into oblivion.

Frank felt the bitter cold snow accumulate against his face as he lay half-conscious, unable to move. The wind pummeled his face with frozen ice crystals ripped from rooftops and sent flying. As he lay shivering in the cold, Frank thought about Katie and the infant she carried in her womb. *It's my baby*, he thought, trembling. *I have to survive this – I'm going to be a father*.

Chapter 31 – Searching for Answers

Laura spent Saturday doing hair and thinking about her early morning conversation with Frank. More than once, she went to the phone to call her roommate and friend, but just as often, she hesitated. She wondered if it were her place to relate Frank's sincere expressions of love and joy to Katie.

After all, she thought to herself, *shouldn't she hear the words directly from him? Frank said he would call in the evening, so what was the harm in waiting? And what if he changes his mind and doesn't follow through with all of his promises? I mean, he's hurt her so bad, running off like he did and not calling her for the last four weeks. Suppose he doesn't call tonight? I don't want her hurt again. I need to protect her. I'll see what happens tonight.*

**

Laura walked in from work, disheveled and exhausted. She threw her keys on the small end table and flopped down on the sofa.

"Oh God, I am so tired," she groaned. "What's for dinner?"

Katie was busy doing laundry and didn't hear her friend enter the house.

"Katie, can you hear me?" she yelled in the direction of the kitchen.

Katie, hearing the shrill voice, turned away from the noisy washer and spotted Laura on the sofa. She walked into the living room carrying a load of semi-wet clothes.

"Hi, I didn't hear you come in," Katie said, reaching for a towel on its way to the floor.

"I'm exhausted," Laura said, exhaling. "I've been on my feet all day – didn't have a single freaking break. Have you heard from Frank?"

Katie looked puzzled.

"Frank – why should I hear from him? He's history. Where have you been?"

Laura bit her lip. *Maybe I was right,* she thought to herself. *Why hasn't he called? I don't understand. He sounded so sincere over the phone this morning. Maybe he'll call later.*

"I just thought – oh well, forget it. I'm so tired I don't know what I'm saying. What's for dinner?"

Chapter 32 – Survival

The wind continued to blow from the northwest sending granules of snow from one unit to another. In the midst of the blizzard conditions, a blue-eyed school counselor lay prone in the snow of his own backyard, a victim of a senseless accident. Frank placed his hands around his left leg, pulling on it, trying to bend his knee. A searing pain shot up his leg as the buried foot was gradually drawn to the surface. Frank clenched his teeth and pulled again. As his shoe came into view, a bloodstained white sock revealed the gravity of his injury.

Frank rolled to his side and dragged his foot away from the sinkhole. He pulled on his parka hood strings, tightening the fur-trimmed bonnet around his head.

Accumulated snow and ice crystals fell to the back of the hood and down the counselor's neck sending cold shivers up and down his spine.

Frank looked ahead trying to judge the distance to the rental office. To the eye, it didn't look that far; getting there was something else. With no way to stand, Frank pondered his plight. His head was on fire trying to control the signals of pain that flashed in a concentric orbit from the ankle to the cortex of his brain. Focusing on anything but pain was almost impossible. Still, he managed to recall his past.

In high school, he'd earned a letter in swimming. The butterfly was his favorite race. The stroke required strong shoulders and forearms. Frank worked hard building his body in those days. With his lean frame, he excelled at the sport, moving through water faster than most of his competitors. As he lay half-frozen, he thought about his swimming prowess and how it earned him the respect of his teammates.

Suddenly the memories took on new meaning. A spark of divinity seemed to appear in the midst of his despair, guiding him into a new plan for survival. He rolled over on his stomach and flung his shoulders up into the air as if in the water. His muscular arms raised up and when they came down, he pushed off on the hard frozen surface. Again, he raised up and pushed off. The former high school letterman looked back to see his progress. A trail of blood marked the distance. He had only moved a foot or so from the storm drain. He looked ahead and judged the building distance at 100 feet. He quickly calculated 200 strokes.

The pain continued to intensify. From the ankle, it made its way up the leg consuming every nerve that could carry a signal to the brain. The pain was excruciating, unbearable and in a strange way, intoxicating. Suddenly, there was a big throb and the pain was gone. Frank reached down and pinched his leg, but he had no feeling. The wind continued to howl, chilling everything to the bone. Frank was losing consciousness. Thoughts of gangrene ravaged his mind as he raised his arms and flung himself forward. He had to keep moving or he would freeze to death. The sound of nylon seams ripping under his arms announced the sheer force of the former swimmer's stroke. By the tenth overhand slap, Frank's hands began to burn. His shoulders throbbed from the sharp impact of his arms against the hard frozen ground.

He stopped and looked back, trying to gain a perspective of his progress. The bloody trail told the story. He had moved just a body length in distance. *No way*, he thought. *I can't make it. I don't have the strength to go on.*

The school counselor's heart pounded heavily and his breathing was heavy. The strain was just too much. Frank laid still in his frozen trail of blood, contemplating his future.

What am I going to do? I have a baby…maybe a boy…he's going to need a father. Katie needs me. I can't let her down.

The thoughts were erratic and primal – those of a desperate soul holding on to life by hope and a promise.

Chapter 33 – Unexpected News

Laura and Katie sat around the small dining room table exchanging glances and sipping mint tea. It was 6:55 p.m. and except for the slight hum of the small chandelier, there was complete silence in the room.

Katie retrieved the last of the dinner dishes and placed them in the kitchen sink. She returned to the dining area to find Laura in deep thought. The silence was annoying. Katie flipped on the TV set in time for the 7 O'clock evening news.

Laura turned her eyes toward the TV set and continued sipping her tea. As she focused on the male news anchor, she thought about Frank's early morning promise to call Katie. *That no-good son-of-a-bitch*, she thought to herself. *I'm so glad I didn't say anything to her.*

It was 7:15 p.m. and the announcer went to break. A commercial came on advertising baby diapers. Katie watched the commercial with more interest than the news. The baby was sitting up and smiling broadly. If the commercial was designed to send a message of delight, it did so and then some. Katie's eyes filled with tears as she thought of the little one growing inside of her. She counted the months till the due date, the date when she too would be changing diapers.

The newscast continued with the reporter talking about local issues. Suddenly, a photo appeared with a caption. Katie's teacup dropped on the floor. The crashing sound immediately called Laura's attention to the screen.

The announcer began his report: 'A former Willamette guidance counselor was found dead earlier this afternoon, the result of an apparent accident outside his apartment residence in Fairfax Virginia. Franklin R. Hardgrove, 24, a former resident of Salem, was found around 4 p.m. this afternoon, about 50 feet from the Fairfax development's rental office. An apartment spokesman said that the teacher had apparently broken his ankle and subsequently froze to death attempting to reach the office. A trail of blood, 50 feet long, revealed a prolonged struggle to reach safety. An investigation is underway.'

Katie's eyes were glued to the screen in horror. Her thin hands were pale, her fists tightly curled, locked in shock. Laura bent down and picked up the broken teacup before reaching out to her best friend. Tears streamed down her cheeks as she placed the jagged pieces on the cleared table. Laura kneeled alongside her companion and placed her forehead against Katie's. The two life-long friends embraced, melding into one. Katie sat cold and distant, unable to cry. She tasted Laura's salty tears as they traveled down her cheeks and onto her lips. The shock of the news left Katie speechless, emotionless and empty.

The sound of the TV filled the room with babble. The reporter's voice droned on as innocuous as the rumbling sound of traffic on the freeway. Laura continued holding Katie. After what seemed like an endless embrace, Laura dropped her arms and pulled apart from her friend. She rocked back on her heels and flicked off the TV. Katie was still staring into space, her brown eyes glistening with tears that wouldn't break loose.

Laura held Katie's hand and brought it up to her mouth. She kissed the hand gently before speaking.

"Sweetheart, I am so sorry. I feel so bad – there are things that I need to tell you, things that you need to know."

Katie looked up for the first time since hearing the news. She looked out at Laura's face and watched the tears that continued to flow from her eyes. *Why is Laura crying so bitterly*, she thought. *I'm the one he ran away from…I'm the one with the baby? Now I have no one.*

Laura wiped her tears with her sleeve while continuing to hold Katie's hand.

"Katie, Frank called this morning while you were asleep. I spoke to him. The night before, when you told him about the baby? He was in shock – which is why he didn't respond to you. You misunderstood his silence and hung up the phone before he had a chance to respond. He was overjoyed to hear the news about the baby. He couldn't believe he was going to be a father. He said that he was going to give up his apartment and his job and that he would be here by next Saturday. He said that he loved you and, yes…that he was going to marry you. He didn't want to wake you so he told me to tell you everything."

Katie looked into Laura's wet eyes and listened to the profound words that would have turned her life around. Suddenly the tears that were held back in disbelief, let go. Katie sobbed out loud as the reality of the situation set in.

"Why? Why didn't you tell me?" she cried out, throwing her hands in the air.

"I didn't know if he was sincere. I didn't want him to hurt you again," Laura answered, her voice breaking. "He said he was going to call you tonight…I didn't see the harm in waiting. I'm so sorry, I didn't know…"

Katie looked down at the ground. She placed her hands on top of her stomach and rocked back and forth, wailing.

"Oh my God," she lamented. "He did love me. He was going to give it all up – just for me…and our baby! I can't believe he wanted to marry me. Why did I hang up on him? Why didn't I trust him? Why didn't I understand?"

Chapter 34 – Confirmation

Katie rose early Sunday morning in preparation for church services at the Mill Creek Mission. She dressed quietly and exited the small cottage a few minutes before 8 O'clock, leaving Laura fast asleep in her temporary bed.

At 9:15 a.m., the phone rang. Laura stirred in her cot. Her breathing quickened at the second ring and by the third, her dark eyes opened wide. She reached across the bed and grabbed the phone. The voice on the other end identified himself and Laura was horribly reminded of the previous night's events. Her nightmare waned as she reached full consciousness.

"Hi," the voice announced. "This is George Secouris, is this Katie?" Laura didn't recognize the name.

"No, this is her roommate, Laura – I believe she's gone to church."

"Oh, well Laura, I don't know if you all heard the bad news about Frank Hardgrove?"

Laura interrupted.

"Yes, we heard it on the news last night, it's just awful."

"Yes, well Frank and I were school chums. I helped him get his job at Arlington High. I couldn't believe it either. His mom called me last night and told me what happened. She told me to get in touch with Katie; she knew about their relationship."

"Did you know too?" Laura asked, stretching.

"Oh yes, Frank talked about Katie all the time. He had plans to marry her, you know?"

Laura hesitated to answer, then said "Oh?" begging for a deeper explanation.

"Oh yeah, he talked about bringing her back East. He loved her very much. A shame it's not going to happen."

"Do you know how he died?" Laura pried further.

"Well it's just like they said on the TV last night. He fell in some kind of hole on the way to the rental office and broke his ankle real bad. They're not real sure, but they think he may have bled to death. We had one hell of a blizzard here yesterday. If he didn't bleed to death, he probably froze out there in the cold."

Laura listened to the explanation of the caller with the southern accent. It brought back memories of her conversation with Frank just the day before. She chided herself again, for not waking Katie.

At least she could have heard his last words, she thought to herself.

"When is the funeral?" Laura asked.

"Mrs. Hardgrove said it would be Wednesday. They're going to bury him in the family plot. Do you think Katie will come?"

"I don't know," Laura answered. "She's pregnant and the doctor might not want her to travel."

"Gosh, I didn't know that," George answered surprised. "Frank never said anything to me about her being pregnant."

"Yeah, well he didn't know until a few days ago. Katie kept it a secret."

"Wow, Mrs. Hardgrove will sure be surprised to hear that. That would make her a grandmother for sure."

"Sure would," Laura replied. "Give me your phone number George and I'll have Katie call you back when she returns from church."

The southerner left his number and Laura hung up the phone, shaking her head in disbelief. Secouris confirmed her nightmare – Frank was really dead.

**

Katie sat in the fourth pew of the small Methodist church, holding the traditional prayer book in her slender hands. Her eyes followed the words of the preacher visually but her thoughts were on the East Coast.

The young mother-to-be looked up at the dark wooden cross, crafted from lumber hewn by community lumberjacks and wondered why God chose to betray her.

Ever since I can remember, I have been going to church and been a God-fearing person. What did I do to deserve this punishment? First my father and now Frank – when will this end? When will things go right for me?

The minister, Reverend Fred Thompson, reached the end of the prayer and moved to the podium to deliver his sermon.

"Dear friends," he said, looking out at the small congregation, "our community is made up mostly of loggers and their families. Just about all of us, including myself, depend on the sawmill for our living. We have invested our hearts and souls in the lumber business and most don't have much to show for it. If we're lucky, we own a small home with a mortgage and maybe a second hand automobile. We live from paycheck to paycheck; a savings account is a rarity."

The preacher paused and looked around the congregation mentally counting the heads and taking notice of those whose eyes were either closed or closing. The congregants numbered 36, about a quarter of the membership. He looked down at his notes and continued his sermon.

"Because of our limited resources, we lead simple lives and for the most part, we accept our plight with dignity. It's rare that I hear complaints about our sub-standard manner of living. On the other hand, when adversity raises its ugly head, in the form of illness, accident or death, there are few of us that don't question our faith. We inevitably ask why God chose us to endure such misfortune.

"The Bible is filled with stories of adversity. The most notable section in the Old Testament is the Book of Job, Chapters 1-42, wherein Job, an upright God-fearing man is suddenly challenged by the evils of Satan. The challenge is basically a wager between God and the ruler of evil to test the faith of Job. This occurs as one by one, Job is stripped of his worldly possessions. He and his family are then afflicted with illness. Finally, all of his children are killed.

"Job reels from the suffering and adversity, curses the day he was born, questions his faith and asks 'why me.' In chapter after chapter, he engages in discourse with friends and God trying to understand God's ways. When he has reached the end of his struggle with trying to understand and, figuratively throws himself upon the heap of ashes, he realizes that all that he has left is his humility before God. He comes to understand that trying to comprehend God's ways is far too complicated for his mortal mind. Once he realizes this, his faith is rekindled and he is spiritually healed."

Holding the edge of the podium with his weathered hands, Reverend Thompson leaned into the wooden platform. He stared into the eyes of his parishioners searching for an emotional connection. Suddenly, his eyes caught those of Katrina. Her eyes were glistening with tears and he knew immediately that his message had touched her.

"What is the message of Job?" he inquired, looking straight at Katie. The question was asked in a rhetorical fashion for everyone knew that the preacher would answer his own question. The reverend stood back and paused. His eyes returned to his notes and he continued his message.

"Job teaches us that life is a battle between good and evil, between righteousness and sinfulness. God represents the good and the righteous while Satan represents evil and sin. Sometimes, Satan prevails and sometimes God prevails. As humans, we are in the middle of these two powerful forces. We can't control either one, but when we understand that God is not to blame for our adversity, we can take comfort in the knowledge that God is good and if He could, He would not allow bad things to happen. In this world, God is not always *all powerful and knowing* and in control. Only in the Kingdom to come, will God's goodness be revealed to us. We will be rewarded not only with eternal life, but also with eternal understanding and truth. That, my friends, is something wonderful and worthwhile – something to look forward to and the true message of Job. May God's goodness prevail over all of you in the years to come and bring you peace. To that, let us say Amen."

Chapter 35 – Katie's Dream

"Katie, Katie, it's okay, everything is all right," Laura whispered softly into her roommate's ear. "You've been dreaming honey, wake up."

Katie opened her eyes but she couldn't see through the blur of tears that flowed down her cheeks.

"Frank, he's dead; he's had an accident...they're going to bury him on Wednesday," she cried out.

"Katie, Laura said a little louder, holding onto her shoulders, "you've been dreaming, sweetheart, you've had a nightmare. Frank is fine," Laura tried reassuring her best friend but Katie was not convinced. She sat up in bed and described her dream in detail.

"We were watching TV and the news came on and they announced that Frank Hardgrove from Salem was found dead in Fairfax, VA." Katie took a deep breath and wiped her tears with her pajama sleeve.

Laura handed her friend a tissue while stroking her hair with the other.

"It's just a dream honey, Frank is fine. He'll be here on Saturday. Don't you remember last night, when I told you that Frank had called?"

Katie tried to recall the conversation with Laura, but her mind was chaotic, filled with images of Frank trying to reach the rental office. She tried to separate the fantasy from the reality but all of her thoughts ran together.

"Yes, I remember talking to you, but I...oh, I am so mixed up."

"It's okay," Laura reassured Katie again. "Give yourself time to wake up. Everything will clear up."

Katie blew hard into the tissue, creating a trumpet-like sound. Both girls laughed out loud.

**

It was almost 9 a.m. on Sunday morning when Katie picked up the phone and dialed Frank's number. An hour had passed since her nightmare ended and even though her mind had cleared, she needed to confirm her sanity.

The phone rang twice before being answered.

"Hello," the voice was strong and upbeat.

"Frank, it's Katie – is it really you?"

"Of course it's me," Frank replied, "who else would it be?"

Katie uttered a sigh of relief.

"Thank God you're okay, I had a horrible dream last night. I woke up thinking something terrible happened to you."

"I'm fine sweetheart, I was going to call you in a few minutes, you know, the three-hour time difference?"

"Yes, I know, so I guess it's around noon there?"

"Yes, I wanted to give you a chance to wake up before I called. Laura told you that I called yesterday?"

"Yes, but she didn't tell me until we were both in bed. I must have been half-asleep. I remember her telling me but then the next thing I knew I was having this terrible nightmare. I remember her saying that you were supposed to call later in the day, but you never called."

"Katie, I did call…around 1 O'clock your time, but no one answered the phone. I assumed you were out. I was so busy making arrangements to come back to Salem, that I didn't think to call again. I'm sorry…I should have tried later."

"No, it's my fault, I should have never hung up on you Friday night. I thought you were angry about the baby."

"Angry? You must be kidding. I am thrilled. I can't tell you how happy you've made me. I should never have left Salem. I reacted too quickly. I promise, I'll never leave you again."

Katie heard the words, but wondered if they were sincere. *How could he love me after the way I treated him and now the baby*, she thought before replying.

"Frank, I'm sorry about everything. I don't want you to feel obligated to me because I'm pregnant. I love you, but you don't have to marry me. We barely got to know each other before you left for Virginia. That night at the inn...well that was horrible and I didn't know what I was doing. Obviously, I have some pretty severe emotional problems and I don't want to..."

"Stop," Frank interrupted. "We'll work everything out. Give me a chance to help you. Babies are supposed to bring good luck and I know that our baby will help to make everything better."

"Oh Frank, you don't know how much that means to me. You don't really have to..."

"Katrina, now just stop that kind of talk," Frank raised his voice. "I will be there with you on Saturday. My flight leaves Dulles Airport at 8:10 a.m. I arrive in Portland around 12:20 p.m. your time."

"Okay, I'll ask Laura to drive me to the airport. What about your car?"

"I've already called Claude. He will leave it on the parking lot for me. Laura can drop you off at the terminal and we'll drive home together in my car."

"Oh Frank, I'm so excited. I can't wait to see you." Katie said tearfully.

"Me too darling, and don't worry about anything. I know everything is going to be fine. I love you!"

Chapter 36 – Saturday

It was 12:10 p.m. and the ground agents were readying the gates for the arrival of United's connecting flight Number-399 out of Denver. Katie stood in the terminal by the giant plate glass window, waiting for the Boeing 737 to make its appearance over the landing strip.

A dark gray cloud cover blanketed Portland's airport. Heaps of snow from the previous week's storm lined the sides of the runway. Shrouds of fog crept along the snow banks making visibility an intermittent study.

The sound of jets revving their engines made it difficult to hear the words of the ground stewards announcing their arrivals.

Suddenly the silhouette of a United plane broke through the low cloud cover, its landing gear down in preparation for landing. From the scurrying going on at the gate, Katie knew it was Frank's plane.

The 200-passenger airliner seemed to float to the runway, its wings extended like a giant bird, gliding ever so gently on currents of air that held the mammoth aircraft aloft until the last moment of descent.

The rubber tires screeched and a cloud of dust blew behind them as the full weight of the plane set down on the landing strip. Within seconds, the whining sound of the jet's reverse thrusters penetrated the plate glass observation window.

Katie breathed a sigh of relief as the giant albatross slowed its forward motion, coming to a rolling stop before turning into the exit ramp.

The plane taxied slowly to the gate, transformed from a beautiful bird in flight to a lumbering ox on the ground.

Conversations quickened in the waiting area as the behemoth unloaded its cargo of passengers. Katie along with dozens of other relatives and friends stood patiently as the passengers made their way up the long dark ramp that connected them with the outside world.

One by one, the men, women and children walked off the ramp into the waiting area, some moving on quickly to baggage claim, while others lingered, embracing loved ones. Katie watched each face pass through the exit, waiting to see the handsome blue eyes

155

of her lover; anticipating his embrace, and the sweet citrus scent of his cologne.

They came in all sizes; short, tall, fat and thin, some with hats and others with canes. Without counting, Katie sensed the last of the passengers. A few stragglers, mostly elderly, made their way slowly up the dimly lit corridor. Katie stood at the gate straining at the remnants of the flight. Finally, two uniformed flight attendants pulling wheeled luggage made their way into the terminal.

She stood there alone, trembling with fear, anticipation and anxiety watching the dark corridor for any further signs of life. The soft brown eyes that had known so much suffering once again filled with tears. Katie turned her back on the ramp and began walking away from the terminal gate, when a voice came out of the darkness.

"Katie, my darling Katie."

***

Epilogue

So, is the voice that came from the darkness of the terminal ramp that of Frank Hardgrove? For Katie's sake, we hope that it is, but what kind of life lies ahead for the troubled young mother-to-be. Is she destined to live out her life, handicapped in her love relationships by repulsive memories of abuse, or will she be able to surmount her destructive past and move on with her life?

A Moment of Passion was written during a particularly difficult year for this author and it is believed that the sorrow reflected in the story parallels that of the author's real-life experience. In the coming year, it is hoped that joy will overcome adversity for this writer, thus providing the impetus for a parallel writing experience in the concluding sequel to this fictional drama.

**

Healthy adult relationships depend to a great degree on healthy relationships learned in the home. Unfortunately, statistics show that many homes in our country foster unhealthy relationships. In fact, government agencies report over a million identified incidences of child abuse each and every year in these United States. By the time these children reach adulthood, is it any wonder that so many adult relationships are flawed?

Order Form:

To order additional copies of this book or others published by Terumah Publishing, please fill out the form at the bottom of this page and mail with your remittance to the following address:

Terumah Publishing
5 Pipe Hill Ct. Unit C
Baltimore, Maryland 21209

The cost of all Terumah published books is $17.00 U.S. postpaid to any U.S. address. All books published by Terumah are sold with complete return privileges. Maryland residents should add 5% sales tax.

Name
_____

Shipping Address
_____

City, State and Zip Code

Indicate number of copies:

Running From Justice: _____
The Minyanaires: _____
Magic, Malice and Murder: _____
Time Passport: _____
A Moment of Passion: _____

Printed in the United States
46831LVS00007B/280-327